HOW TO HUNT A HUSBAND

HOW TO HUNT A HUSBAND

HOLLY JACOBS

Ilex Books 2019
ISBN: 978-1-948311-03-8

Originally published
Harlequin Books
Copyright © 2003 by Holly Fuhrmann.

TABLE OF CONTENTS

REVIEWS

"Holly Jacobs is at the top of her form in this hilariously funny romance. The dialogue is snappy and her characters would be right at home on "I Love Lucy." ... This is a delightfully funny read, and a sure pick me up.

~Romance Junkies

"Sure to please, Holly Jacobs's HOW TO HUNT A HUSBAND (4) offers a unique and hilarious take on the classic 'fake fiancé' plot."

~RT BOOKclub

"This story is a laugh riot! It is full of witty banter, charming characters, and plans gone awry. Everything comes together to form the perfect tale with just the right amount of everything one desires in a romantic comedy."

~© Loves Romance

"HOW TO HUNT A HUSBAND showcases Jacobs at her outrageous best."

~Word Weaving

How to Hunt a Husband
Holly Jacobs

"That woman," Brigit O'Malley said.

There was a certain humph in her mother's voice that left no question in Shannon O'Malley's mind as to who *that woman* was.

Tuesday was pinochle day, so *that woman* had to be Cecilia Romano. Even a beautiful March day—and beautiful days in March were rare and treasured in Erie, Pennsylvania—couldn't obscure the black cloud *that woman* had given Brigit O'Malley.

Actually not much could shake Brigit from her Tuesday evening funks.

"Mom, why do you go play cards every week when you always come home in a snit?"

"I am never in a snit. *Snit.* That's such an undignified word. I am—" her mother paused a moment, searching her thesaurus-like-brain for a better word choice. "Perturbed. Cecilia perturbs me beyond the limits of what a sane rational human can endure. Why, do you believe she's saying her daughter could—" she sputtered her way to a standstill.

"Cara?" Shannon said. "What could Cara do?"

Shannon didn't actually know Cara Romano, but knew of her, not only through their mothers, but because

1

Shannon's sister, Kate, had married Cara's ex-fiancé, Tony Donetti.

The logistics of their connection was tangled at best, but it was their mothers that made Shannon feel a bond to the unmet Cara. After all, Cecilia Romano seemed as determined to control the fate of her children as Shannon's own mother was.

Thankfully Brigit O'Malley had long ago decided that Shannon was a hopeless cause and had concentrated on getting Kate's life in order. But since her sister had moved to Texas with her new husband, Shannon had noticed her mother was around a lot more, dropping in unexpectedly—like she'd done this evening—and taking a sudden interest in Shannon's activities.

Truth be told, all the attention made Shannon a bit nervous.

More than a bit.

A lot.

Her mother stopped sputtering and said, "Cecilia said Cara can find a man before you can, when everyone knows that you are far more beautiful than that Cara Romano is. Why men are beating down your door, begging to marry you … aren't they?"

"Not exactly."

Beating down her door? Heck, she could hardly remember what it was to have them knocking softly.

Shannon hadn't had a date in months. She'd been so busy planning for Kate's wedding, then dealing with her parents in the aftermath of her sister's great bridal escape, that she simply hadn't had the time—or inclination—to date.

"And, since I'm not looking for a man, Mother, I'm going to assume that Mrs. Romano is right, Cara will probably beat me to the alter."

No, the last few man-free months had convinced Shannon that dating was overrated. Without a man in the picture she'd been able to do exactly what she wanted, when she wanted, without having to consult someone else. She hadn't watched one blood-and-gut-testosterone-filled film during the entire time. She'd watched chick-flicks. Lot's of chick flicks. She'd drooled over Colin Firth, Ewan McGregor, and Hugh Jackman—big-screen men who didn't mind that she hadn't shave her legs for weeks.

Yes, there were advantages to a man-free existence.

"I think in the future I'm only going to date men on a limited basis. *Limited*, Mom. That's the keyword. I'm not looking for anything long-term when I date from now on. I've decided that I want to see a man only as long as the initial politeness lasts."

"Initial politeness?"

"You know, that golden time in a relationship where a man will do what you want. When he'll listen to what you have to say, as if every word is a treasure. Why, when things are new he'll even see chick-flicks or go shopping. Once that glow is over, I'm done with him.

That was going to be her new rule of thumb. *Use them, then lose them.*

"Shannon Bonnie O'Malley, you take that back."

Shannon suppressed a shudder. "Mother I hate it when you call me that."

"We've had this fight over and over again. Bonnie is a perfectly lovely name. It was my mother's name and she was a wonderful woman. You're lucky to be named after her."

"You're right. Bonnie is a perfectly lovely name, so is Shannon for that matter. But some names don't go together. Bonnie doesn't go with Shannon. Ichabod and Archibald, they don't go together either."

"Why do you have to be so difficult? Mary Kathryn never complained when I called her Mary Kathryn."

That was the refrain of her relationship with her mother. Shannon had been *difficult* when she'd played soccer rather than join the science club. She'd been *difficult* when she'd discovered a passion for art rather than something more academic.

Her sister was the good daughter. Her sister had bent to her parents' dreams for her.

And Shannon? Well, she was the variable in the equation of her mother's life.

"Ah, but Mary Kathryn's not a Mary Kathryn anymore, is she?"

When her sister ran out on her wedding she changed her life completely. New man. New state. New job. New name. A part of Shannon envied her sister those changes.

"She's Kate. Kate Donetti," Shannon continued. "And I think she's happier that way."

Her mother just shook her head. "You are the most difficult, cantankerous girl alive."

"I learned from the best." Shannon leaned over and gave her mother a peck on the cheek. She'd never really seen eye-to-eye with her about, well, about anything, but she loved her.

And though she frequently annoyed her mother, she didn't doubt Brigit loved her as well, even though she wasn't overly demonstrative.

"Here, try this on," her mother said as she thrust a garment bag at Shannon.

Shannon looked at the huge bag.

"What is this?"

"It's Mary Kathryn's wedding dress. I asked her to mail it back to me. We spent a small fortune on that dress, you know. I want to see it walk *all* the way down the aisle. Oh, she did some damage we'll have to get repaired, but let's see if it fits you before we worry about that."

"Fits me?" Shannon stared at her mother, not sure where she was going with this. "Why would you care if it fits me?"

"Well, if it doesn't we'll have to get it altered or find something else for you to wear." Her mother put her hand on Shannon's shoulder and started steering her toward the bedroom. "Come on, try it on."

Shannon ground her heels into the carpet and faced her mother. "Wear when?"

Maybe her mother's fight with Cecilia had finally driven her over the edge. Maybe she'd been sniffing just a bit too much formaldehyde in the lab she worked at.

Maybe her mother was totally deranged.

"At your wedding," her mother said.

"What wedding?" Shannon asked feeling not-very-bright and more than a little nervous.

"The wedding I'm planning. I told you what Cecilia said about Cara. I can't let that woman beat me, so that means I can't let her daughter beat you to the altar. I thought right after school got out. June twenty-fifth. What do you think about that day? That leaves you plenty of time for a honeymoon before you start back to school next fall. Of course that doesn't leave me long to get the entire thing planned. Less than four months."

"Mother, I know I seem dense here, but just who is it that I'm supposed to be marrying?"

Shannon had often felt like the not-so-bright family member. Her parents and her sister all had a ton of initials behind their names. They worked in academia.

Well, actually, since she'd married Tony, Kate worked in Donetti's Irish Pub and Cooked Sushi Bar, but that was

5

beside the point. She still had initials behind her name, and Shannon was still *just* the high school art teacher.

Oh, her family never added the *just* to her job description, at least not out loud, but Shannon knew they thought it. They valued those initials, and though she had a BA in education and art, she didn't have all those extra, more impressive initials. And she taught art, not a serious subject like science.

Shannon realized her mother was talking again. Something about a wedding.

Her wedding?

Who did her mother think she was going to marry?

"… Seth."

Shannon's attention jumped back into focus. "Mother, you're not suggesting I marry Seth? You went to his wedding to Desi, after all."

"How could I forget? Why, when it was Mary Kathryn's wedding that wedding planner didn't worry at all when I pointed out the cake was too small, but at her own wedding? Why the cake was huge. A veritable mountain of cake. Still I never understood why she had Barbies on the top."

Her mother was quiet a moment, obviously pondering why Seth and Desi had Barbies for their wedding cake toppers.

"So what does Seth have to do with anything?" Shannon finally asked when she couldn't stand the silence any more.

"I called Seth to see if he knew a nice man you could marry…"

Nathan Calder sat at the bar in O'Halloran's Bar and Grill. He wasn't drinking anything harder than cola even though it was Friday and he was off tomorrow. He'd simply come to show Mick how he'd spent his tax return...on his new Harley.

Yep, he was a bad-ass, Harley riding...pharmacist. A bad-ass, Harley-riding pharmacist who'd only just got his motorcycle license and obviously shouldn't have been awarded it, since he'd stalled the motorcycle three times on the way over to Mick's.

He felt like he was this year's April Fools joke because it was hard to feel tough when you were sitting in the middle of traffic, wearing your new leather jacket...and trying to restart your engine.

Harder still when you flooded the engine and had to wheel the motorcycle to the side of the road and wait ten minutes for the gas in the carburetor to evaporate before you could restart it.

Nate took a sip of his cola, wondering how he was going to get the bike home without repeating the incident.

He planned to ride the bike to hockey practice this week and let his team *ooh* and *ah* over it, but maybe he should rethink that plan, at least until he'd mastered the art of not stalling.

Nate caught a glimpse of movement out of the corner of his eye and turned. A beautiful woman took the seat next to him. A heart-stopping, beautiful woman. Tall, with reddish hair cut short, but not the least bit mannish. No, this woman was the type who made any man in proximity sit up and notice.

The kind of woman who made him forget all about his Harley-troubles.

"Hey, Mick. Could I have the usual?" she called in a husky sort of voice that made every man within hearing distance who hadn't already noticed her, turn her way.

7

"Sure, thing, Shannon-me-love," Mick said in his patently fake Irish accent.

"Come on, Mick. Give the lady a break," Nate ribbed his friend. "You know you grew right next door to me in Glenwood Hills, not in the green hills of Ireland."

Nate shot a grin at the redhead.

The bartender smiled as he said, "Ah, sure I do, Nate, but Shannon likes the brogue for atmosphere, don't you my sweet?"

"Ah, Mick, the-Irish-apple-of-my-eye, you can be sure I do. Why, if me mum keeps insisting I get married, I may just take you home and make the poor woman's dreams come true. Why, she'd not only be getting her wedding, but it would include a good Irish boy as well. Ah, she'd never recover from the sheer joy of it all. And I'd be trading the O'Malley last name for O'Hallaran. My initials would stay the same. Yes, you may be the perfect husband material … at least if it wasn't for the wee fact that you're a hound when it comes to the women."

Mick leaned across the bar and said, "And though I'd rather be kissing a banshee than marrying anyone, I might just make an exception for you, Shannon-me-love."

Chuckling he moved toward the other end of the long bar where a customer was hailing him.

"He's something else," Shannon murmured as she took a sip of whatever it was Mick had given her.

"Sure is. Why, his first day of high school he convinced the teachers he was an Irish exchange student."

Mick's Shannon grinned as she asked, "You knew him then?"

"Sure did. We've been friends forever. I'm Nathan Calder. Not that he'd ever introduce me to a pretty lady. He likes to keep them all for himself. Selfish, that's Mick." He chuckled and added, "Friends call me Nate."

"Shannon, Shannon O'Malley."

She held her hand out to Nate and they shook.

If asked, Nate would have testified that there were actual sparks flying off their joined hands. He'd have sworn to it in a court of law. Slightly bemused by the experience, he pulled his hand back as quickly as possible.

As a professional, Nate had shaken a lot of hands, but none that left him feeling as *shaken* as Shannon's did. It wasn't as if there was anything special about her hand. He quickly glanced at it to make sure.

Nope. There was nothing special about it at all. Just five fingers, on a nicely shaped palm. One small ring. Short, neat manicured nails.

What on earth was he doing noticing a woman's manicure? He must be more flustered than he thought about the whole stalling the motorcycle thing.

He tried to pull his scattered wits back together. "Well, Shannon-me-love O'Malley, if Mick stands you up on that offer of marriage, give me a call. My mother would love nothing more than to hear some woman is making an honest man of me."

"You're mother's on the marriage kick, too?" she asked, sympathy in her voice.

"Not just the marriage-kick," he admitted, "but the grandbabies-kick as well."

It wasn't that Nate didn't like kids.

Someday he might want one...maybe even two. But not now. After all, he'd just bought a Harley. Harleys didn't come with baby-seats. Plus it was hard to be a bad-ass biker if you were carting around a diaper bag.

Okay, so it was hard if you couldn't go more than three blocks without stalling the motorcycle, but it would be worse with a baby, of that he was sure.

"Oh, mine hasn't started in about grandchildren yet," Shannon was saying. "No, she's just after a husband for me. She's already planning the wedding in June."

"Oh, so you do have a fiancé?" he asked, slightly disappointed. After all, he'd noticed the ring on her hand, but it wasn't on the correct finger. He sighed. Here was a woman he would have liked to get to know better.

Not in a marrying, baby-producing way, but in a she's-too-hot sort of way.

He'd love to feel her body pressed against his, his Harley rumbling beneath them as they rode through town. And after the ride… Well he could think of a few other places he'd like to take this woman.

"No, there's no fiancé," she said. "But that's not going to stop my mother. Why she's already set the wedding date and is calling around trying to find a priest who will marry us since Father Murphy said no. Fortunately, all the rest have said no as well, since there's no groom. Priests have rules about that kind of thing. And my mother wouldn't consider me really married if I wasn't married by a priest in the Church, wearing a long white gown with a whole group of her friends watching."

"You win hands down," Nate said. "My mother just complains about her lack of grandchildren." His voice rose and he said, *"And to think of the forty-eight hours I spent laboring with you. The doctors said another baby would kill me and so you were destined to be my only one. An only child who almost killed his mother."*

"Oh, she brings out death-guilt? That's a hard to battle fight," Shannon said.

"It gets worse." Again he altered his voice and said, *"And all those years I slaved away, trying to be the best mother I knew how to be, and all I want from you now is grandchildren before I'm too old to enjoy them. But do you care? No. Every girl I introduce you to you find something wrong with. You're too picky, that's what you are."*

"*Too picky.* My mother says the same thing. She's spent the last month fixing me up with…well, between you and me, I don't think she's been *picky* at all about the men she's hooked me up with. Desperate. That pretty much describes my mother's match-making."

She sighed and took a sip of her drink. "Tonight's date was a prime example. I told her no. No more dates. I have plans, you see. I want to live a solitary, chick-flick, hairy-legged life. But she invited me out to dinner with her and my father. At least that was the story. They were at the restaurant, all right, but so was he. His name was Neil. He works with Mom and Dad at the college."

"Doing what?" Nate prompted.

"A philosophy professor. Mom and Dad had a mysterious lab emergency. Have you ever heard of a lab emergency?"

Nate shook his head.

"Me either. Anyway, they left Neil to entertain me while we finished eating."

"You don't look overly entertained," Nate said with a chuckle.

Frustrated. That's how she looked.

Nate could sympathize. His mom had planned her own set-ups these last few months.

"Oh, Nate, you don't know the half of it. Neil spent the rest of the dinner talking about things so deep my head was spinning. It's not that I'm dumb, but he was intentionally being pompously difficult. Then he turned the subject to how Kepler's observations of heavenly bodies impacted our way of viewing the world around us, and added that he'd like a chance to spend more time studying my heavenly body…"

Shannon drained her glass. "Well, I finished my spare ribs faster than anybody should and I hope Neil was feeling philosophical about my emphatic rejection of his heavenly-body proposal. There was absolutely no way I was *impacting* with him."

"Most men aren't overly philosophical about rejections," Nate pointed out.

"Yeah, he didn't seem very pleased. My mom called my cellphone to apologize for their *emergency* and to see how the rest of the meal went. I told her that I left right after the entree because I didn't want to be Neil's dessert. That's when she accused me of being picky and I said if she didn't watch it, I'd show her how non-picky I could be by picking a man that would fry her butt. I mean a biker, with long greasy hair, and tattoos, or something. She'd be off my case about marriage quicker than she could light a Bunsen burner."

"Yeah, rebellion has its place. My mother wants me to grow up and settle down, though maybe not quite as bad as your mother wants you to. Mom keeps pointing out I'm thirty and that it's time to become an adult. But to be honest, I don't recall ever having a childhood, so I've staged my own mini-rebellion. I've decided it's time to do some of the things I've always wanted to do but was too busy with school or establishing a career to try."

Nate took a sip of his cola and continued. "I thought about tattoos, as a matter of fact, but I didn't think it would go over well with my customers."

"Customers? What do you do?" Shannon asked.

Nate smiled and replied, "I'm a pharmacist. I can't see my customers being comfortable with me tattooed. And you? What do you do when you're not out on bad dates?"

"I'm a high school art teacher."

"Too bad you weren't a stripper or something. I could take you home and scare my mother out of rushing me into marriage."

"Yeah," Shannon said, wistfulness in her voice. "If only I was a stripper and you were a greasy-biker, life would be perfect."

They both paused and though he didn't know her well, he could see she realized the opportunity they had in front of them at the same moment he did.

Nate weighed the possibility. After all, he didn't need an actual stripper. He just needed his mother to *believe* he'd brought home a stripper.

"I just bought a bike," Nate said slowly. "A Harley Fat Boy."

"You did?" Shannon asked, something akin to awe in her voice.

Nate nodded. "So if we told your parents I was a biker, it wouldn't actually be a lie."

He didn't mention the fact that he still questioned his abilities to actually ride the bike.

"And I do take my clothes off every night to put on pajamas, so I guess you could say I strip."

They both laughed and let the idea grow. "You know, if I took you home disguised as a stripper and told my parents I was in love with you—a woman who takes off clothes for a living—my mother might get off my back about babies, at least for a while."

"Your mother would hate a stripper daughter-in-law as much as my mother would hate a biker son-in-law."

She grinned. "Oh, it's too perfect. Kismet even. My mother would have to rethink her wedding plans if I brought you in and introduced you as the man in my life. The only man I'd even consider marrying."

Nate thought his mother was a bit of a pain, but Shannon's mother sounded certifiable. "Um, you didn't really explain why your mother is already planning your wedding, even though there's no groom in sight."

"Well, it all started when my sister—the good daughter— ran out on her wedding with the best man. She changed her name from Mary Kathryn to Kate, and changed her man from Seth to Tony. She also changed careers."

"From?" he found himself asking, even though he wasn't sure he was following Shannon's explanation.

"From research scientist and professor, to employee at Donetti's Irish Pub and Cooked Sushi Bar."

"Cooked sushi?" he echoed.

Maybe it wasn't just Shannon's mother who was crazy…maybe it was her whole family.

"It's a long story," she warned.

"I've got all night. And we'll need each other's full stories if we're going to entertain this plan."

Shannon took a deep breath and started, "Well Mary Kathryn and Seth were best friends who decided to marry because it seemed like the logical thing to do…"

Nate half-listened to Shannon's story unfold. The rest of his mind was occupied wondering just how she'd looked dressed up like a stripper.

The mental images were tantalizing.

This might be a crazy plan, but desperate times called for desperate measures.

And this mental image of Shannon disguised as a stripper was making Nate feel quite desperate.

CHAPTER TWO

"Nate, is that you?" Judy Calder called out as Nate entered his parents' home the next morning.

Normally Nate would have to suppress a groan, knowing the course his conversation with his mother would be taking.

It wasn't that he didn't love his mother. Of course he loved her. Loved her a lot. After all, how could you not love a woman who almost died giving birth to you?

But this week the only thing he was suppressing was a grin.

He followed the sound of her voice into the kitchen. "Yeah, Mom it's me. Where's Dad?"

His father could generally be counted on to run interference on the grandbaby nagging front, not that Nate wanted too much interfering today. He had the plan, after all.

A delightful plan.

A perfect plan.

A mother-proof plan.

A plan guaranteed to buy him some much needed respite from his mother's pleas.

"Your father was on call and had to run into the store," she said.

"I just stopped in to check that little leak you were having under the sink," he said from the doorway.

The kitchen was next-to blinding. Bright yellow walls, brilliant white cabinets, sparkling surfaces. A floor you could probably actually eat off of.

Judy Calder believed in everything being just-so, whether it was her kitchen or her son's life.

She turned from the counter. In her late fifties, his mom didn't look her age at all. Slim and brunette, she was often mistaken as Nate's sister when they were out together.

They might find his mother was young looking, but no one ever mistook his father, Paul Calder, as his brother. His dad had been grey since Nate could remember and he blamed his wife for every one of those grey hairs. But years of watching how much his father doted on his mom, Nate suspected it was merely genetics, because the two of them were obviously meant for each other.

"Oh, honey, that's so sweet of you to stop and see about the sink. But it's okay. I called a plumber. After all, you know you're not any more mechanical than your father is."

He opened the small door off the kitchen that led to the laundry room and grabbed his father's toolbox from the corner.

"Not mechanical? Mom, how can you say that? After all, who fixed the dryer just last week?"

"You kicked it, dear."

"It stopped making the noise right after that."

His mother didn't understand the finer art of home repair. Nate's opinion was, when something worked, don't fix it, and when something didn't work, try kicking it first. In this case, kicking was all that was called for.

"Why it was practically purring when I finished," he said as he set the toolbox down on the counter and opened it up.

His mom shook her head and kissed his cheek. "And it started squeaking again about ten minutes after you left.

I got out the spray lubricant, unscrewed the back of the machine and sprayed all over. It hasn't squeaked since."

"It was my kick that took care of it."

His mother looked ready to contest the point, so he hastily went on, "But, I won't argue. Just let me have a look at the sink. If I don't think I can handle it, we'll just let the plumber come. But do you know how much they charge for a service call?"

Slowly, his mother backed away and gave him room to open the cabinet doors. Nate rolled up his sleeves and slid down and under the sink.

"Probably not as much as the roofer charged when he had to fix your patch job," his mom muttered.

"I heard that," Nate called as he studied the silver U-ish pipe over his head.

"I wanted you to. And speaking of hearing, I need you to listen. No excuses that you didn't hear me this time. You're coming to dinner Friday night. It's Sunday, so that's five days notice."

He wiggled the U-ish looking pipe. "This seems loose. Hand me the big pipe wrench, okay?"

She handed the wrench to him as she continued, "About dinner on Friday. I'm going to invite Jocelyn and her daughter Kay over."

"No."

Too bad he couldn't kick the pipe. He could barely get his torso under the sink. But he gave it a couple good thwacks with the wrench just in case that was all it would take. But the pipe just seemed even looser after that and not fixed at all, so he tried to get the wrench around the big bolt that held the sections together.

"And I'm going to make that pot roast you like," his mom continued.

"I hate pot roast. I like pork roast and sauerkraut."

His mother always forgot what his favorite dishes were. He thought it was some passive-aggressive way of getting back at him for not giving her grandchildren yet.

"And I'll make some of my delicious homemade dinner rolls."

"They're like bricks."

"And you're going to love Kay—"

"Kay? Couldn't her parents give her a whole name? Kay. I could never love a woman who's name was just an initial."

"—and maybe she'll be the one you finally marry. Then the two of you will give my grandbabies. Lots and lots of grandbabies. I've met Kay. She's built for babies. Wide hips, you know."

He thought of Shannon. He wouldn't call her hips wide. Not that they were too thin. No, they looked perfectly proportioned to the rest of her body.

His mother would be disappointed.

He grinned—thankful he was hidden under the sink—ready to launch the plan he and narrow-hipped Shannon had devised. "Sorry mom. Kay sounds delightful. But I'm seeing someone."

"Since when?"

He could hear the suspicion in her voice.

Deciding to stick to the truth when possible, he said, "Last night, at Mick's place. They're friends."

"You met her in a bar? Nice girls don't go to bars and pick up men," his mother assured him.

"She didn't pick me up, I picked her up."

Mick had practically had to throw them out so he could close because they'd sat and talked so long. The plan was simple. They'd use each other as a weapon to diffuse their mutual mothers' matrimonial designs.

18

One bad-ass biker and a stripper to the rescue.

"Well, nice girls don't let men pick them up in bars," his mother humphed.

"This one did."

He finally got the big pipe wrench to grip the bolt that connected the pipes and turned it.

The pipe fell off with just the first half turn and landed on Nate's nose. "Ow!"

"What did you do to my sink?" his mother yelled.

"Your sink?" he hollered back and he shimmied out from under the cabinet, gripping his aching, moist feeling nose. "Your sink? What about my nose? I think it's sunk into my face."

"I always thought your nose was too big anyway. It could use some sinking. You have your father's nose, and he doesn't have an attractive one."

"Thanks, Mom." Nate grabbed the towel held it to his nose, trying to stem the flow of blood. "Can you bleed to death from your nose?"

"No. Now what about my sink? You broke it didn't you? And now the plumber is going to charge me twice as much."

"Mom, I'm dying and you're worried about your sink and money? That shouldn't be the biggest concern of a devoted mother. My bleeding to death should be."

She folded her arms across her chest, obviously not feeling overly devoted. "What did you do to my sink?"

"The bolt that held the pipes together was obviously loose, which is probably why it was leaking and it explains why it fell off so easily. I'll just tighten it back down and you should be fine."

"That's what you say. But I remember that time you were going to cut down that tree in the backyard. You broke my chain saw."

"Mom, I'd cut almost all the way through that branch and was trying to pull it down when that big one over top of it fell instead … you're lucky it crushed the saw, not your son."

"Well, I was rather partial to that saw," she said with a mischievous grin. "Let's face it honey, though I adore you, you're not very handy."

"Gee, your faith in me makes me feel special. And speaking of feeling special, I've got a new girl now, so you can cancel Friday night's dinner with the wide-hipped, initial girl."

Maybe just mentioning a new woman would be enough to get his mother off his case for a while. If it worked, they wouldn't have to move on to the second part of their plan.

"No, I won't cancel dinner," she said. "Though I won't invite Kay. Instead you can bring this bar floozy to meet your mother."

She lifted the towel and peeked under it as his nose. "I think it stopped bleeding, but you're going to have quite a mark."

Nate gingerly felt his nose, and though it seemed swollen, it didn't feel as if he'd broken it.

"Wonder how the floozy will feel about your new nose," his mom added.

"She's not a floozy, exactly. She's a nice girl."

"Who got picked up in a bar."

"Mom, our first official date's Friday. You don't take a girl to dinner at your mom's on the first date."

He grinned. Arguing with his mother was a part of the plan. After all, if he gave in too easily, she'd suspect something. She was a sly one, his mom.

But he was slyer.

Much slyer.

Why, if he hadn't become a pharmacist, he probably could have been a spy, he was so wily.

"Maybe you should bring over more first dates. After all, you've never brought one here before, and I still have no grandbabies. Maybe if you bring this girl here now, she'll realize you're serious about this relationship."

"You said she was a floozy. Why would you want me to be serious about a girl like that? And who said I was serious? It's our first date. We just sat at the bar and drank last night, so that doesn't count. If I bring her here for dinner she'll think I'm—"

"A nice guy," his mom interrupted. "She'll think you're a nice guy. Dinner will be at seven. Don't be late."

She leaned over and glanced under the sink. "Now fix my sink."

If he'd become a spy instead of a pharmacist he'd name his missions. He thought of possibilities as they started to reattach the pipe.

Operation Meddling Mothers. Yeah, that was perfect.

Operation Meddling Mothers was about to begin.

"Mom?"

Shannon had already agreed to Sunday dinner with her parents—and no one else—before she met Nate. She had expected to find the ordeal trying. But now, despite her mother's new *marry-off-Shannon* campaign—or rather because of it—she was looking forward to the evening.

"Oh, Shannon there you are. I have so much news. I've been busy," her mother said as Shannon walked into the house at promptly four-thirty.

"Me, too," she said, kissing her mother's cheek.

Her mom patted the chair next to her. Shannon sat as her mother exclaimed in an excited, breathless voice, "I'm sorry that your dinner with Neil didn't work out."

"Mom, you have to stop setting me up. I'm not interested."

As if Shannon hadn't even spoken, her mother continued, "I've got you a date for next Saturday night! A nice boy. His name is Shelby."

"Sorry, Mom, no can do."

"Now, Shannon, there you go, being difficult again. I know you have name issues and you think I haven't thought about how Shelby and Shannon sound together. But I have. It's not a Shannon-Bonnie thing. Oh, I know, I know you're going to say that whenever someone says your names together, other people with think they're being shushed, but really, dear, that's a very narrow view. A man is more than his name."

"Mom, really it's not his name—"

"And I know that you think this entire wedding thing is just about my bet with *that woman*, and maybe that's what instigated it, but Shannon, dear, let's face it you're not getting any younger. It's time you settled down and found happiness. Why your father has endowed my life with such joy. I want you to find a man as endowed as he is."

Shannon started choking. "Mom—"

Her mother, obviously unaware of what she'd just said, continued, "And I realize that you like to buck the system. That you hate to do anything I suggest because…well, because you're just a tiny bit difficult, dear."

Shannon was about to argue that she might be difficult but she'd learned from the best. And not only was her mother difficult herself, she was certifiable. But Shannon didn't get to say all that because her mom held up her hand, stopping her before she started.

"Uh, uh, uh. You know you are. All I'm saying is don't say no to meeting Shelby just because I suggested it. I'm not saying marry him tomorrow—"

"No, you're saying marry him in June."

"At the end of June," her mother corrected. "That gives you plenty of time to get to know him. But that's not what I'm worried about. I'd just like you to meet a nice boy. Shelby's a podiatrist. He's—"

"Mom, if you'd take a breath, I'd tell you I can't go out with Shelby because I'm already seeing someone. It's not because of the name issue, though you're right, that would be the pits."

"See, I knew the name thing would be an issue," her mother muttered.

"It's not the name thing. It's simply that I've thought about what you said the other day, about me always fighting your wishes, and I've decided you were right. If you want me to consider marrying, I will. As a matter of fact, I've found a man I really like. We have a date next weekend."

"Really?" Her mother looked suspicious.

"Really," Shannon assured her. "Mom, we might not always see eye-to-eye, but I never lie to you. Yes. I met a man after I ditched Neil. His name is Nathan Calder and I like him."

That wasn't a lie at all. She did like Nate. Oh, there was a physical attraction. After all, the man gave new meaning to the phrase *tall, dark and handsome*. But it was more than that. He genuinely seemed like a nice guy. Easy to talk to. Down to earth.

Why, they'd sat at O'Halloran's and talked most of the night away. Mick finally had to kick them out.

But they'd made good use of their time. They'd devised a plan to take care of both of their mothers' nagging.

If Shannon was looking for a man—which she wasn't. She was sticking to her motto, use them and loose them. But if she was, Nate might warrant a look, or even two.

"I think you'd like him," she said.

Silently she added, *if you met the real him.* But if things went the way they'd planned, Brigit O'Malley wasn't going to like Nathan Calder at all.

"You'll bring him by?"

"Yeah. Next weekend sometime, maybe? Let me run it by him and I'll get back to you about when."

Shannon spent the rest of the visit basking in her successful first step. Her mother was about to learn a valuable lesson. *Be careful what you wish for… it just might come true.*

Oh, yeah. Her mother wanted her to find a significant other, and Shannon was about to do just that.

Only Shannon doubted that when her mother envisioned her riding away, duly wed, that she pictured her on the back of a Harley.

Shannon Bonnie O'Malley, who would have thought?

Shannon asked herself the rhetorical question as she stared at her reflection in the mirror.

She was rather awed by what she saw.

Oh, Shannon had realistic views of herself. She wasn't gorgeous, but she wasn't so ugly that her-mama-tied-pork chops-around-her-neck-to-get-the-dog-to-play-with-her when she was a baby. She was comfortably in the middle most days.

But now?

Well, who knew that the right undergarments could make such a difference?

After she'd hatched her plan with Nate the other night, she'd made an emergency trip to a lingerie store to prepare for their date and had left herself at the mercy of the sales clerk there.

The woman and her underwear—not *her* underwear, but the underwear the store sold—were amazing.

Panties that sucked things in.

And a bra that stuck things out—things she never even imagined she'd own.

Actually, the bra was the most interesting contraption she'd ever seen. It had a little pump and she could actually inflate it until she'd achieved just the right size breasts.

Oh, they were fake breasts, but—she checked the mirror again—no one would ever know. Instead of a flat drop from her neck to her feet she had a long channel of cleavage exposed from the daring cut of her new red dress. A new red dress that would give her mother a heart attack and convince Nate's mother that pushing for grandchildren might not be such a great idea, at least not if Shannon was the woman in the running for becoming their mother.

She backed up so she got a good look at the entire effect. Though the hemline fell to her knees, the slit up either side practically showed off her new body-sucking panties.

Oh, yeah, this was good.

She finished applying her make-up with a heavy hand and studied the results.

Yes, she believed she could convince Nate's mother she was a stripper.

No, she took that back.

Not *stripper.*

If she was a stripper, she'd find the term insulting. Degrading even.

Even if she was a taking off her clothes for money, she hoped she'd still retain her sense of dignity.

Exotic dancer.

Yep, that's the term she'd prefer if she was a stripper...exotic dancer. It sounded so much more dignified.

Her doorbell rang and she checked her watch. Nate was prompt. She liked that in a man.

She slipped on her stiletto-heeled boots and zipped them all the way to her knees, then hurried to the door.

She opened it and immediately looked to Nate's face for his reaction to his exotic-dancing date.

His slack-jawed, ogling response was just what she'd hoped for.

"I take it you approve?" she asked.

"Oh, honey, I do, but my mom will absolutely faint. She told me only floozies allowed themselves to be picked up in a bar and when she gets a look at you, she'll rest her case, but she won't rest easy. As a matter of fact, after seeing you, my mother might try to make me move back home so she can protect me."

"Do you think you need protection?" Shannon asked her throatiest voice. She figured if she were an exotic dancer, she'd have that kind of sexy bedroom-voice and had been practicing all week.

"I don't think any man in his right mind would want to be protected from you. But I do think every man's mother would want to lock them up rather than let a stripper like you—"

"Actually I prefer the term exotic dancer, if you don't mind," she said, pleased she'd managed to keep a straight face.

She'd managed, but Nate didn't.

He burst out laughing.

"Oh, that's good. Real good. You know, you could have been an actress instead of a teacher."

"Well, it won't be good if you laugh like that. How are we supposed to convince your mother you're head-over-heels in love with me if you can't stay in character?"

"Sorry." He crossed his heart. "It won't happen again."

"It had better not. It's not just that I'm worried you'll blow the charade with your mom. That would be your problem, after all. It's that I need to know you're going to be able to convince my mom when we go meet her tomorrow."

"I don't know if I'm ever going to be able to look as good as you do."

"I'm going to take that as a compliment."

"You should. But can I point out that Shannon isn't a very good stripper name."

"Oh, I thought about that. When I dance—I'm an exotic dancer, not a stripper, I'll thank you very much to remember that—I use the stage name Roxy."

"Oh, Roxy is good." He laughed. "I think you're having just a little too much fun with this."

Shannon drank in the sight of him—and oh what a sight it was. Nate had that Cary Grant-ish sort of look—the kind that was born for a business suit, but could as easily carry off just jeans and a t-shirt.

She wondered what he'd look like in a tux.

She tried to picture it.

Oh, yeah, Nate Calder would look mighty fine in a tux. His shoulders were broad and the jacket would hang ever so comfortably from them.

As a matter of fact, she thought she'd tuck quite comfortably under those arms, given a chance. Not that she expected to be wrapped in Nate's arms... not unless they had to because of their act.

But if she did get tucked into Nate's arms, she thought she'd fit well.

Wrapped in Nate.

The mental image of him holding her so tight that she could hear his heart disappeared when he said, "So let's go. We don't want to be late for my mother's dinner. Though I hope you heeded my warning and ate something already. My mother might be known for her lobbying for grandbabies, but she's not known for her cooking—especially her pot roast."

"That bad?" Shannon asked.

"Worse."

Nate's Harley was parked outside her apartment building waiting in all its regal splendor. "Oh, wow, this is a great bike."

He puffed up. "It's a classic. A Fat Boy. I can't believe how lucky I was to find one."

He handed her a silver helmet. "Will it mess up your hair too much?"

"No. There are advantages to short cuts. I'll just spike it back up when we get off."

"Then come on."

Climbing on the back of a motorcycle wearing stiletto heels was more difficult than Shannon had imagined. She used Nate's shoulder to steady herself.

He stood and pressed down on the starter.

The engine turned over, but didn't catch.

He did it again.

And again.

Nate turned around and offered her a sheepish grin. "Sorry. I just got my license, and I haven't quite got the hang of some parts of motorcycle riding yet."

"Would you be insulted if I offered to start it?" Shannon asked.

She didn't want to hurt his feelings. Despite their bravado, men tended to be rather fragile egos. "I've been riding motorcycles since high school. I dated Johnny Palmer, the school's resident bad-boy and he taught me."

That wasn't all Johnny taught her. One night when he got a bit too presumptuous and Shannon had slugged him hard in order to convince him that no meant no. She'd learned to hitch-hike because Johnny up and left her on the side of the road.

"You ride motorcycles?" Nate asked.

"I don't own one, but I do know how to ride."

"Can you start one in those heels?"

She grinned. "Let's see."

Nate climbed off the bike and stood next to it as Shannon slid up into the driver's seat.

She stood and pressed on the starter. The motorcycle hummed to life with a Harley's belly-rumbling sound.

"There you go," she said, her voice loud in order to be heard over the noise.

"Why don't you just drive?" he asked.

"Are you sure?"

She peeked at his face and he seemed serious. Most men she knew wouldn't be caught dead buzzing around town on the back of a motorcycle driven by a woman.

Women might have come a long way, but Shannon had found that not all men had.

"Sure I'm sure. I tend to stall it...a lot. And mom will have a fit if we're late. But maybe later you could give me some lessons?"

Oh, Shannon could think of a lesson or two she'd like to share with Nathan Calder, but she didn't share that bit of information with him.

Their dates were completely for show. They were cohorts, nothing more. And of course, she wasn't looking for more. Why, she wanted to revel in her chick-flick watching, hairy leg, single status.

Not that her legs were hairy tonight. The dress was too high cut for that. But as soon as they'd derailed their mothers' wedding plans, she was going back to not shaving…at least not too often.

"Let's go," he said.

She simply nodded, and let him crawl onto the bike.

Nate's arms wrapped around her stomach. The top of his right hand grazed the bottom of her pumped enhanced breast.

Shannon found herself wishing there wasn't a balloon full of air separating her breast and his hand. She'd like his hands—

She cut off the thought. She wasn't in a real relationship with Nate. They were conspirators. Associates.

Despite his Cary Grant-ish looks, she had to remember that.

"Here we go," she called as she pressed the pedal, put the Harley in first gear and took off down the street, ready to begin the game.

Chapter Three

"Mom, we're here," Nate called as he opened his parents' front door and walked into the living room with its lime green walls and slate grey carpet.

Over the years Nate had gotten used to his mother's loud color choices and rarely gave them a second thought. He actually kind of liked things bright and a bit wild. But he saw the surprised look on Shannon's face and wondered if she preferred something more sedate.

No, she didn't look like the sedate type in that dress. She looked like a pin-up girl ... a fantasy woman.

Not that she looked like *his* fantasy woman. No, she looked like every man's fantasy. That dress. He forced himself to concentrate on the job at hand, which was convincing his mom to lay off the wife and baby stuff.

Shannon's dress was a means to an end, that's all.

"Mom? Dad?" he called.

"Come on, they must be in the kitchen."

Shannon stood and nervously smoothed some invisible wrinkle in her skirt.

Gone was the illusion of an exotic dancer named Roxy, and in her place was an art teacher who was feeling nervous.

"What's wrong?" Nate asked softly.

She sighed. "They're not going to like me."

"They're not going to like me dating a stripper."

That was the plan. His parents wouldn't like her and her parents wouldn't like him. No more marriage talk.

"Exotic dancer," she corrected, as if she'd been doing it for years.

Then, softer, she added, "People normally like me."

"Shannon-me-love," he said, using Mick's pet name. "We don't have to do this. Come on, it was a crazy idea anyway."

This was supposed to be fun, but Shannon didn't look as if she was having fun. Not at all.

She gave herself a little shake and said, "No, no, I'm okay. Just chalk it up to a case of stage fright. It's not a crazy idea… well, maybe it is. But we have crazy mothers, and it's sort of like fighting fire with fire… fighting their craziness with a crazy plan of our own."

She straightened and smiled at him. "Let's go."

"Shannon, really you don't have—"

"Come on, big guy. Roxy never misses an entrance."

She smiled and Shannon the art teacher was replaced by a stripper—an exotic dancer, he corrected himself—named Roxy.

"You're sure you can pull it off?" he asked.

"You just watch and learn, biker-boy." She patted his cheek. "I'm going to show you how it's done. Don't forget, you'll be putting on your own performance tomorrow."

He turned and heard noise coming from the kitchen. "Well, I'd say its show time."

His mother rounded the corner.

"Nate," she said, spying him, her face one big happy smile… until she spotted Shannon.

The smile disappeared rather abruptly and was replaced by something that looked like it could be terror.

But Nate would give his mother credit, she held out her hand, stuck a fake looking smile on her face, and said, "You must be Nathan's new friend."

Shannon took the hand and shook it a bit too enthusiastically. "Oh, it's so nice to meet you, Mrs. Calder. I mean, most guys don't take me home to meet their moms even after we've been dating for a long time, but Nate here, he's brought me on a first date. You know, the minute he walked into the bar, I knew he was something special."

"Ah, yes, the bar," his mom said just as his father walked into the room.

"Paul, this is Nate's friend—"

Nate was pretty sure he heard a sound akin to horror as she said the word friend.

"—uh, dear, I'm not sure I caught your name."

Shannon laughed, a throaty sort of laugh.

Nate wondered if it was part of her act, or just her normal laugh. He couldn't tell and wasn't about to ask. He preferred to think it was part of the act.

"Shannon, ma'am. Shannon O'Malley, although at work I go by Roxy."

"At work?" his mom asked.

"Yeah. My boss, he says Shannon doesn't give a man the right sort of mental image, and mental images are our specialty."

"Just what do you do, Shannon," Nate's father asked.

Nate just stood back, waiting for the shoe to drop.

Shannon grinned. "Why, I'm an exotic dancer. Didn't Nate tell you?"

"What?" his mother gasped.

His father didn't say anything. He just stood, looking from Nate and back to Shannon.

"An exotic dancer," Shannon repeated.

"A stripper," Nate explained.

Shannon elbowed him...hard. "I told you I don't care for that term. It sounds dirty. I do what I do because I'm good at it, because I need to earn a living. It might not be the Rockettes, but it's not raunchy."

"A stripper?" his mom said weakly.

"It's a nice place, ma'am. The owner, well, he doesn't let anyone mess with the girls. He looks after us. Hey, we even get medical insurance, and you know how expensive that can be. Why my friend Candy—her real name is Patricia, but the boss says that doesn't create a good mental picture either, so she's Candy at work—why she's got two kids. Her deadbeat husband left her, and doesn't pay child support or anything. So she works the morning shift—"

"Strip joints have morning shift?" Nate's dad asked.

"Ours does," Shannon said, her head bobbing as she nodded. "Twenty-four hours a day, seven days a week."

"Uh," Nate's mom said. "Dinner is ready, so why don't we all go in and sit down."

Nate took Shannon's arm and they followed his parents into the dining room.

"You're doing great," he whispered.

"Yeah, I am," she whispered back and shot him a grin.

Yes, Nate could see his mother's immediate baby plans fading fast. She would never want a stripper for her grandchild's mother. Yep, Shannon was doing a great job, playing the stripper to the hilt.

But as the meal went on, Nate realized things weren't going quite the way he planned.

Shannon went on talking about the strip club, about Candy and her two kids, about Marcy, the exotic dancer who was working her way through grad school. She wove intricate tales that had the entire family hanging on her every word.

Nate hardly noticed the charbroiled nature of the roast his mother served or the huge lumps in the mashed potatoes. He was as caught up in Shannon's stories as his parents were.

"Why," she said, leaning across the table, exposing cleavage Nate hadn't noticed at the bar the night they met—and he was man enough to always notice cleavage, so how had the fact that Shannon had some escaped his notice?

"One night," she said, "I was up doing my number and was down to just panties and tassels, when this guy comes in and jumps up on stage. Now, my boss, he doesn't let anyone mess with us, and no one is allowed on stage, so Bruno—he's our bouncer. I asked once and his name really is Bruno, which seems a bit to stereotypical to me, but it's his last name, not his first. His first name is Kyle, which isn't bouncer-ish at all. Anyway, Bruno—he'd kill me if I called him Kyle—he jumped up and grabbed the guy before he could touch me. And the guy lunges forward and makes a grab anyway, but all he grabs is a hand full of tassel, which means I was left there exposed..."

She paused for a moment, and if Nate didn't know it was an act, he'd have sworn she was truly embarrassed by the incident, as if it had really happened.

"Oh, dear, what did you do?" his mom asked.

"Well, of course, I covered myself. I mean, I strip, but only to tassels and panties—we don't strip all the way—and here I was one tassel shy of a complete outfit. And then, this guy he tosses me up his jacket, and before you know it, there was a pile of jackets and shirts at my feet. Why I just picked one up, slipped it on and finished the dance. You should have seen my tips that night."

"Why, the men were gentlemen," his mom said, a note of approval in her voice.

HOLLY JACOBS

If Nate didn't know better, he'd have thought his mom was almost impressed.

"Most of the guys who come in are gentlemen. Sort of lonely. Part of the job is going out between sets and visiting them. Most of them are just happy to have us there, talking to them. I feel sort of bad for them."

Man, she was playing this as the stripper-with-a-heart, not the heartless stripper.

Nate glanced at his mom. She'd always been a soft touch, and one look at her face told him that she'd fallen for Shannon—aka Roxy's—story.

"Why, dear, I never thought of it that way. Why else would a man go to someplace like that? Of course he goes because he's lonely."

Nate could swear he heard his mother sniff.

Shannon had his mother believing that not only was she a stripper, but that she was a stripper with a heart-of-gold, dancing to help a bunch of lonely, sweet gentlemen.

"Not all the guys go there because they're lonely, Mom," he felt obliged to point out.

"Of course that's why they go," his mother said.

"The poor men just don't know how to interact with women," Shannon, the arm-chair-psychiatrist, said.

"Why, maybe we should start some sort of support group. Men who visit strippers—"

"Exotic dancers," Shannon corrected.

"Exotic dancers," his mother agreed. "We could see if we could find a therapist, and you could take brochures to work and hand them out to the men. Why, we could teach them how to deal with women in the real world. How to meet nice girls."

"Hey, we're nice girls," Shannon said.

"Why, of course you are, dear. But you're already dating Nathan, and the one girl's in grad school—between that and work, she doesn't have time for a relationship—and the other one has young children and a nasty ex. The gentlemen at the club have problems. We need to introduce your friends to men who don't have too much emotional baggage of their own—someone who can help them deal with theirs. We can—"

"Mom, you'll put the club out of business if you reform all its customers and save all its dancers," Nate said. He gave Shannon a little kick under the table.

"Nate's got a point," she said. "My boss is a nice guy and runs a clean club, but I don't think he's nice enough to let us lose all his business for him. I'm sure he wouldn't allow me to pass out brochures."

"I guess you're right," his mom said with a sigh. "But I think I'll talk to some people in town about setting up a support group, anyway. We won't target just your club, that should work, shouldn't it?"

"I—"

"Honey," Nate's dad said, "I think you're putting Shannon on the spot. This is her first dinner with us, after all. There will be more."

"You're right, Paul. Shannon, we'll talk about this later, next time you come. Right now, let's talk about dessert. I made Nate's favorite, Key Lime Pie."

Nate forced himself to smile as his mother looked at him expectantly. "Great."

Great. Just great.

His mother had implied she expected to see Shannon at dinner again, which meant she liked her.

His mother liked Shannon in spite of the fact she thought she was Roxy, the exotic dancer.

And, in addition, they were having his *favorite*, Key Lime Pie, for dessert.

Nate hated Key Lime Pie.

"…Yes, Mother." Shannon sighed heavily, on purpose, so that the sound would carry over the telephone wires.

"I heard that, young lady."

"Heard what?" she asked, though she knew the answer. It was better to play this out. After all, her mother had to believe she was reluctant to bring Nate over to the house.

"That sigh," her mom said, right on cue. "Is it so much to ask that I meet this man? You said you'd talk to him about stopping in."

"Talk to him. I said I'd talk to him. I didn't say we'd stop in for sure. If you just wanted to meet him that would be one thing, but you want a wedding and you're assessing his ability to play the groom—that's another thing entirely."

"Now, Shannon, you know that I only want what's best for you and—"

"Have you talked to Kate this week?" she asked.

If she were really trying to get out of bringing a man to meet her mother, she'd try to sidetrack her.

"You're changing the subject," Brigit accused.

Shannon was glad her mother couldn't see her broad smile. It was useful to know someone so well, especially when trying to put one over on them.

"No, no I'm not," she denied. "I just wondered if you'd talked to her."

"No." Her mother's voice was laced with suspicion. "I was going to call her after I talked to you."

Shannon smiled. Her strategy was to keep her mother off-balance and she had a bombshell all ready to drop and topple her. She fired. "It seems Cara's in Texas."

"Cara's in Texas?"

"Yes."

"Now, why do you suppose she's down there? Are you saying you think it's something to do with her mother? That Cecilia sent her down there? Maybe she thinks Cara will have luck finding a cowboy. Goodness knows, the girl wasn't finding a man here in Erie."

"If Mrs. Romano is taking this bet as seriously as you are, I wouldn't be surprised if they're up to something."

Shannon didn't add that she didn't think Cara would be any more happy about this bet than she was.

"After all," she continued, "if they tried something in Erie, you'd certainly find out. But Texas… that's a big state. Who knows what the two of them have cooked up."

"Well, I suppose I'd better call Mary Kathryn—"

"Kate," Shannon corrected her mother.

"Kate," her mother said with a sigh, "I'll call her and see if she knows just what's going on."

"That's great. Goodbye, Mom."

She didn't get the phone a millimeter from her ear before her mother yelled, "Oh, no. You might have given me something new to worry about, but I haven't forgotten that I expect you to bring the boy—"

"Man."

"—to the house for dinner tonight."

"Mom, we just met. It's just a date."

"Good," her mother said. "Dating is good. Bring him by and we'll find out all about him together."

"I'll bring him along if you promise not to start talking about weddings with him."

Silence.

"Mom?"

"Fine. I won't mention the word wedding. Now, be here at five. I'm calling Kate."

"Five it is, Mom."

"I look forward to it," her mother said right before she hung up.

"So do I," Shannon murmured to herself as she hung up the phone.

At least she hoped she did. After all, last night hadn't gone the way they'd planned.

She admitted it was her fault.

She'd apologized to Nate, and though he'd accepted her apology, he'd still been a bit put out when he'd dropped her off at home.

Shannon knew where the problems stemmed from. It was a curse.

She liked to be liked.

She blamed genetics.

Women were trained to be likeable, to be easy-going. They were genetically and socially predisposed to want to be accepted.

No, that might sound good and scientific, but unfortunately the theory just didn't play out.

Look at her mother. She obviously didn't have an overwhelming compulsion to be liked. Not that Shannon didn't like her mom.

She did.

But easy-going wasn't a phrase that people used to describe Brigit O'Malley.

Overbearing.

Pushy.

Opinionated.

Competitive.

But not easy-going.

And frequently not likeable.

No, wherever this need-to-be-liked thing stemmed from, she couldn't blame her mother or her mother's genes.

But she could blame her mother for the fact she found herself in this absurd situation at all.

Her musings were interrupted by a sound that could only be a Harley Davidson. Loud and rumbling, the Harley drew closer, and Shannon's heart sped up.

Not that she was excited about seeing Nate.

Of course she wasn't.

Her accelerated heart rate probably had to do with the fact she was nervous that he was mad at her.

Not that she'd blame him if he was.

A tiny part of her had been afraid he wouldn't show up today. Not that she cared on a personal level—they hardly knew each other after all, though she was inclined to like what she did know of him.

No, the only reason she was concerned about his not showing was because she needed him to get her mother off her back.

And now, he had shown up, even after she'd mucked up last night. Maybe he'd only shown up because his mother had invited her back to dinner next weekend. Well, she'd use that time to try to undo the damage she'd done last night. She was going to carry her exotic dance routine as far as she could and try to shock his mother into disliking her.

She wasn't going to examine the fact that knowing she'd be seeing Nathan again next weekend wasn't any particular hardship.

Shannon waited for him to knock, even though she knew he'd arrived. Heck, with the amount of noise the

Harley made, the whole neighborhood knew he'd arrived. But she didn't want to appear too ... excited? Anxious?

Whatever.

She just didn't want him thinking she was too pleased to see him. She was playing it cool, despite the fact her heart was racing and her palms were sweating.

She heard the knock and had the front door opened a split-second after his knuckles tapped the wooden door.

Nate jumped back half of a step, obviously startled that she'd opened the door so fast.

So much for her cool act.

"Hi, Nate," she said, trying to gauge his mood.

"Shannon." He didn't smile and her name came out rather terse.

He was still upset.

Darn.

"Aw, come on, Nate, I said I was sorry. I swear, by the time dinner is over next weekend, your parents will be begging you never to see me again. Your mom will declare she can wait to be a grandmother, at least until you find an appropriate woman. I'm really sorry that they liked me."

His hard expression evaporated and she saw a hint of a smile. "Well, it was kind of funny to hear her go on about starting a support group for guys who frequent strip-clubs."

Shannon chuckled. "By the time I was done describing the place, I almost believed I was talking about other exotic dancers, and not just adapting stories about teachers I know from school. I never realized I had a gift for telling stories."

"Blarney," Nate said.

"What?"

"Mick would say you have the gift of the blarney. A fine Irish tradition."

"Well, if anyone knows blarney, it's Mick. I can see why you've kept him around all these years. He's a great guy. I'm not much of a bar person, but after all my mom's fix-ups, I always seem to end up there. Mick's doesn't seem like a bar, but rather just a place to hang out with friends."

Something in Nate's expression changed slightly. Oh, he was still smiling, but there was some difference that Shannon couldn't quite identify.

"So are you ready for our lesson?" he asked, not sounding overly enthused.

They'd agreed it would be better if Nate was the one driving the motorcycle when they pulled up to her parents, so she'd suggested they spend the afternoon practicing.

Shannon figured if she could teach kids to appreciate art, she could teach Nate to ride a Harley without stalling…at least she hoped she could. That way when the charade was over he'd not only have his mother off his back, but he'd be able to actually ride his motorcycle.

"I'm all set," she said. "I thought we'd go over to the school parking lot. It's virtually deserted most weekends."

"Fine. You drive there, I'll drive back."

CHAPTER FOUR

*H*e's *a great guy.*
An hour and a half later, Nate was still stewing about Shannon's comment about Mick.

It wasn't as if he didn't agree. Mick was a great guy.

Funny.

Intelligent. He'd been working his way through school for years. Balancing his schoolwork with owning his own business—so you could add independent to his glowing list of *great*ness.

Yeah, Mick was a great guy, and all of a sudden, it bothered Nate and he wasn't sure why. Oh, he might suspect, but he wasn't sure and wasn't about to examine his level of annoyance until he was sure. He was afraid of what he might find.

Because there's no way he could be jealous.

That flood of *some feeling* that overtook his system every time he thought of the casual friendliness Mick and Shannon had displayed the first night had to be something else entirely.

A great guy.

Ha.

He could tell Shannon some stories about great old Mick that would make her spiky hair stand on end. But he wouldn't because who Shannon thought was *great* made no difference to him. It wasn't as if they were anything more than partners. He had no real claim on her.

Why, he hardly knew Shannon.

They were just helping each other out of their mother-marriage woes.

She could date whoever she wanted. Not that she was dating Mick.

At least, he didn't think she was dating Mick.

Maybe he should talk to Mick and make sure Shannon wasn't dating him.

Not that it mattered.

It wasn't as if Nate was looking to date Shannon in any way except their *fake* way.

He eased the motorcycle into her driveway and cut the motor. She unwrapped her arms from around his waist.

He sort of missed the feeling of her pressed against him.

"That was great, Nate," she said as she climbed off the bike.

She pulled her helmet off, set it on the back of the bike and ran her fingers through her short hair as she grinned at him. "You made it all the way home without stalling it once. I think you've got it."

"Thanks to you." Nate put down the kickstand and leaned the bike gently against it, then took off his own helmet.

"Nah. You would have got it on your own. You just needed practice, that's all."

"What time are we supposed to be at your parents?" he asked.

"Five. We've got time."

"Time for what?" he asked. There was a certain gleam in her eye that made him nervous.

They'd talked about motorcycle lessons and dinner, but they had no other plans for the day, of that he was sure.

"Time for me to take you to see my friend, Emilio."

Emilio?

How many men did Shannon have hanging around?

"Is he a great guy, too?" Nate asked.

The moment the words were out of his mouth he wished he could suck them back in.

"What?" Shannon asked, shooting him a piercing look with those beautiful green eyes.

Beautiful green eyes? Man, next thing you know he'd be waxing poetic about her emerald gaze or some such nonsense.

"Never mind," he said, his voice sharper than he intended. "So, why are we seeing this Emilio?"

"Because you're getting that tattoo you wanted," she said with a grin.

"I don't think so," Nate said, feeling a hint of regret.

It's not that he hadn't toyed with the idea of a tattoo, but it certainly didn't fit his daytime persona and ... well, he didn't like needles.

It wasn't a very manly concern, so he didn't confess it to Shannon, but there it was. It wasn't just a small dislike, but more of a minor phobia.

Okay, maybe a major phobia.

Yeah, he was not meant to be tattooed.

"No. No tattoos."

"Trust me," Shannon said.

"So what do you think?" Nate asked as he climbed off the motorcycle he'd parked right on her parents' perfectly manicured lawn.

Oh, her mom would hate a Harley on the lawn, which is why she'd told Nate to park on it.

Shannon stood at the side of the motorcycle, dressed in the most preppy and innocent looking outfit she could manage. A pale blue oxford shirt, a dark blue pair of jeans and white tennis shoes. She wanted to dress in stark contrast to Nate's outfit.

She'd helped him pick it out and thought they'd done a great job transforming her professional looking pharmacist into a bad-ass biker.

Nate was dressed in a black t-shirt with its arms cut off, and a black leather vest.

Okay, so his hair wasn't long by anyone's standard, but he'd done something to it. It looked wild. He'd put on dark glasses that shaded his warm brown eyes. Well-worn, faded black jeans and black leather riding boots finished the ensemble.

Well, almost finished.

"So?" He flexed his arm and the mermaid on his right forearm undulated in a suggestive sort of way.

It was fake, but no one would know it.

Emilio was good. Fantastic, actually, she thought with a great deal of teacherly pride. She'd been working with him privately for a few years. He was one of the best artists she'd ever seen.

The crowning glory of her year was getting him an art scholarship. It felt like a validation for all the time and effort she gave to both her school students and her private ones.

She loved teaching and helping kids learn to appreciate art, while she worked with ones who not only appreciated it, but created it. Occasionally there was one of those rare students who had the type of raw talent that just begged to be developed.

Emilio was one of those.

"My mother's going to freak out," she said, admiring Emilio's work. "Mom's not into guys with tattoos. She's hoping for a professional for me. Let's see, she's fixed me up with her banker, her accountant, and even tried to fix me up with her gynecologist... I drew the line with that one. Ew. She thinks I need someone who will settle me down."

"So, she's hoping for a professional. What are you hoping for?" Nate asked from the other side of the motorcycle, suddenly serious. He peered over the top of his dark glasses, waiting for an answer.

"Someone I can love." The words out before she could stop herself. She could feel her face heat up. What a stupid, stupid thing to say. "I didn't mean to say that."

"You're embarrassed," Nate said. "Why would wanting to be loved embarrass you?"

"It sounds so ... I don't know, juvenile. But it's the truth. I want someone special. I'm not settling for less than love just because my mother might lose a bet. I want what she has with my dad, what Kate found with Tony."

"Good for you." They walked toward the front door.

Before they reached the steps, she stopped. "And you? What are you looking for?"

"I don't know. I don't think guys spend much time thinking about stuff like that."

"If you don't think about it, how are you going to know what you want?"

"I guess I'll figure it out when the time comes."

Shannon found his answer less than satisfactory, not that it mattered what Nate was looking for in a woman. Didn't matter a bit. All she was worried about was this meeting with her parents.

"What you're looking for doesn't matter tonight. What does matter is that you're looking to be as shocking as possible. I want my mom to send that dress back to Kate. I want her to not weigh every man she meets as potential husband material for me. I want her to cancel the church and stop hounding local priests."

"I'll do my best," he said with a grin.

They walked up the steps and onto the porch. The boards creaked as they walked across it to the door.

Shannon knocked, rather than just unlock it with her key and walk in. She was staging a grand entrance, after all. It wouldn't work unless someone was there to witness it.

"By the way, Roxy," Nate said with a devilish grin, "I have a new name, too, don't forget. Bull."

Shannon snorted. "Yes, that's good. Very biker-ish. I'll remember to use it."

"I thought you'd like it. I—"

Nate was interrupted as the door flew open.

Shannon's mom stood there, a smile on her face ... a smile that slowly faded when she saw Nate.

"Shannon?" she asked, still staring at Nate as if she couldn't look past the biker on her steps to see if her daughter was indeed present. She didn't even notice the motorcycle on her front lawn, she was so horrified by Shannon's date.

"Hi, Mom," Shannon said brightly, pleased with her mom's reaction. "This is my friend, Nate, Nate Calder."

"But call me Bull," he said. "That's what my friends all call me. I think it fits my personality better than Nate ever did."

"Bull?" Brigit asked weakly.

"Yeah."

Shannon saw the moment her mother spotted the motorcycle. If anything she looked even more horrified.

"And is that your ... vehicle?" her mom asked, her voice even fainter.

"My bike? Yeah. Isn't she a beaut? A bike is like a woman, they each have their own personality, their own style. It takes just the right man to ride them. My bike, like Shannon, is a lady. A classy ride. I can't figure out why either of them like me, but I'm glad they do."

He loped an arm over Shannon's shoulder and pulled her toward him.

She'd been right when she'd figured that she'd fit easily within the confines of his embrace.

"Oh, Bull," she murmured as she batted her eye lashes in what she hoped was a love-sick manner. "You do say the sweetest things."

"They're not always sweet," he said with a suggestive lilt to his voice.

"No," she said with a grin that suggested a private joke. As if she suddenly realized her mother was there, she added, "Oh, Mom, I'm sorry. It's just that Bull makes me forget myself."

"Oh," was her mother's flat response.

"Are you going to invite us in?" Shannon pressed.

"Certainly. Certainly. Come in." Brigit didn't add *make yourself at home.*

As a matter of fact, she wore an expression that said she wanted to go lock up all the valuables before Nate came in the house.

Somehow Shannon kept a straight face. Nate did as well. He was doing fantastic. She'd have to do as well next week when they went to his parents and redeem herself for yesterday's little *like-me-fest.* She had a week to learn to be difficult and as unlikeable as possible.

"Your dad's out back grilling some steaks," her mother said, as she led them through the living room and into the dining room. "You do like steak, Mr.—"

"Bull. Just call me Bull, Ma'am. And of course I like steak. A real manly meal, that is. I was afraid we'd be eating some highbrow sort of meal, like couscous or sushi. Give me a big steak any day of the week. Rare, if that's okay."

"Rare. I'll tell Sean," Brigit said as she hurried out. "Shannon make your friend at home."

The minute her mother was out of the room Shannon started laughing.

"*Bull. Just call me Bull, Ma'am*," she mimicked. "You're good, Nate. Very good."

"I thought she was going to pass out," he said.

"Me, too. She went to get my father for reinforcement. That's unusual. Normally Mom likes to run the show unimpeded. You must have her flustered if she's going for help."

Shannon got Nate settled at the dining room table and brought him a beer.

"I don't like beer," he said.

"Drink it. It's part of the persona," she whispered, just before her mother came back into the room, her father in tow.

"Bull," her mother said, barely hesitating on the name, "this is my husband, Sean. Honey, this is Bull, your daughter's date."

Oh, Shannon had truly upset her mother if she was being designated as *your daughter*. The only time that happened was when she or Mary Kathryn was really in the doghouse.

Shannon watched as her father set the steak down and her mother fussed with drinks. They kept shooting each other looks. It was that strange *couple-speak* that some couples—couples who were truly connected and meant for each other—had. Those kind of looks carried more meaning than words.

Shannon knew that she'd never marry for less than what her parents had. She wanted someone who could read her looks, who understood her. Who would support her.

She wanted someone who would love her.

Why couldn't her mother understand that?

Her parents had set the relationship bar extremely high. But Kate—the perfect daughter, the daughter who even when she rebelled managed to still retain her perfect status—had emulated her parents' relationship when she'd married Tony Donetti.

Oh, maybe they didn't seemingly have as much in common as her parents did—at least not on the surface—but it didn't take much to see that they fit together perfectly.

They'd given each other looks like her parents shared when they came home for Seth and Desi's wedding. Shannon had noted those looks and envied each one.

No matter how hard her mother tried to marry her off to an acceptable man, she was going to hold out for an *exceptional* one.

The dinner was quiet for a while, then obviously Brigit couldn't stand it any more because she said, "So, Bull, what do you do for a living?"

"Oh, a little of this and a little of that," he said in a noncommittal way around the bite of steak in his mouth.

"Which means?" Brigit pressed.

"I only work when I have to. And I've done a bit of everything. A bouncer. Mechanic. A few jobs I don't think I'd better bring up." He chuckled as if he'd said something funny, but Shannon's parents didn't even crack a smile.

"So…" her father finally said when the silence at the table grew too weighty, "How did you two meet?"

Shannon looked to Nate giving him the floor.

He obviously caught her meaning, because he said, "We were introduced by a mutual friend at the bar, then we went to an art show and that's when I knew Shannon here was the woman for me."

Shannon figured her parents would totally freak out at the bar comment, but instead her mother zeroed in on the second part of his statement. "An art show?"

Shannon was glad her mother asked, because she'd love to know just what Nate had in mind with that little tidbit.

"Yeah. There was a local show of Biker Art."

"Biker Art?" her father echoed.

"Yeah. All the tattoos this local artist has done over the years...he'd taken them all, and copied them onto canvas collages."

"Tattoos?" her mother said weakly.

"Yeah. I have a lot of them, though this mermaid," he flexed his arm, causing the mermaid to wiggle suggestively, "is the only one that shows unless I take off my shirt," he paused half-a-beat and then added, "or pants."

"Oh, no," her mom said in a rush, "that's fine. The mermaid is beautiful."

"Yeah, I think so. As a matter of fact, Shannon here is thinking about getting a tattoo with me. Matching hearts with each other's name in 'em. Maybe we'll do that as an engagement thing. What do you think, Babe?"

"Engagement?"

Her mom just kept repeating what Nate said, as if she was too shocked to think of anything original to say.

"Yeah," Nate said as he reached over and patted Shannon's hand on the table. "Shannon here, she told me about how you need her to get married in order to win a bet, and of course, I'm willing. I mean, if anyone understands how important winning a bet is, it's me. I've probably won, and then lost, a million dollars over the years. I'd like to see to it that you win because, let's face it, that's a lot more fun than losing. After all, you'll be my mother-in-law soon, so your honor is tied to my honor and I wantta see you win."

"But married? Why you only just met," Brigit protested.

"Shannon said you had everything reserved for the end of June. That leaves us plenty of time to get to know each other."

"But…but…" her mother stuttered.

Shannon stared, mouth slightly agape. Her mother was stuttering. That never happened. Her mother was always in control, always had a plan, always had some contingency, always got the last word.

Nate had totally silenced her mother.

He was her hero.

She reached under the table and gave his knee a squeeze of thanks.

"Shannon," her mother said with a tsking noise. "Are you two teasing? Married? Already? Oh, you two. I want Shannon to marry for compatibility, stability—"

"Love?" Shannon added.

"Of course, love. I would never want you to marry so I could win a bet."

Shannon managed not to scoff.

Bull smiled. "Well, Shannon and I were sort of set on the idea of a June wedding, but we could put the final decision off for a while, if that would make you feel better. Just don't go canceling anything 'cause I can't see me changin' my mind."

"Definitely put off a final decision for a while," her mother echoed. "It wouldn't do to rush into things."

"But Cara's in Texas and Mrs. Romano—" Shannon started.

"Shannon, the ideas you get. I was just kidding about the bet."

"But Kate's dress?" Shannon asked.

"You'll have it when you need it, but I don't want you to rush into anything."

"But—"

"So, Bull, why don't you tell me more about…" her mother hesitated as if searching for a subject she thought was safe. "Your motorcycle."

"Well…" he said, and launched into a long monologue of the joys of Harley Davidson motorcycles. As he talked he gave Shannon's hand another squeeze.

She just sat back and watched her mother's wedding dreams evaporate.

It was a good night.

CHAPTER FIVE

"Good night," Nate, aka Bull, said when they arrived at Shannon's house a few hours later.

Shannon was riding a high because they'd defeated her mother.

She'd won.

She swore she watched her mother's wedding-dreams fade into nothingness as the night progressed.

"You could come in for a while, if you like," she said.

Nate looked surprised to hear the invitation, which is exactly how Shannon felt when she heard herself issue it.

She wasn't sure why, but she was sure she wasn't ready for the night to end.

"I don't have work tomorrow," he said, slowly, almost hesitantly.

What was with him?

Nate had been quiet since they left her parent's house. Not that it was easy to talk on a motorcycle, but still, he seemed ... well, distant.

"Never mind," she said. "Forget I asked."

She was just asking him in to celebrate their victory over her mother's defeat and you'd have thought she was asking him to get his teeth drilled.

"No, I mean, yes, I'd like to come in."

He might have said the words, but they didn't sound overly sincere.

Did she have cooties or something? She'd been sweating bullets at the beginning of the evening, but she didn't think she smelled.

"Really, never mind. It was just an idea," she said as she unlocked the door and stepped inside.

She would have shut the door in his face, but he caught it before it shut and pushed it back open. "Shannon, I'd really like to come in."

She shrugged and started walking into the foyer, leaving the door open for him to follow if he wanted.

She didn't turn around, but heard the door shut, and then his footsteps against the hardwood floor as he followed her into the house.

"Make yourself at home," she said, gesturing toward the couch.

This room was the reason she'd bought the house. Big, with dark, original woodwork, a huge stone fireplace and hardwood floors. She loved nothing better than to curl up on her couch and just enjoy the comfort of the room.

But tonight, with Nathan standing in it, the room didn't feel big, or comfortable.

"Do you want something to drink?" she asked after he'd taken a seat.

"I'm okay. Those couple beers were plenty."

She wished he had wanted something so she would have an excuse to leave the room and collect herself. For some reason, she was feeling a bit breathless and she wasn't sure why.

She sat opposite of him on the couch, leaving as much space as possible separating them.

Silence weighed heavily on the room.

Shannon tried to think of something to break it and finally said, "Um, I don't suppose you're hungry?"

"Nah. Your mom's a much better cook than my mom is, only don't tell my mom I said that. I'm quashing her grand-baby plans, I don't want to take everything away from her."

"Okay."

Silence again ruled the room for what seemed like an eternity.

Finally, Shannon said, "This is silly. Just go home. It's okay."

"No it's not okay," he said, turning to face her. "What's going on? Even that first night, we didn't have any trouble talking to each other. I felt an immediate connection. As if we'd been friends for years. So why all the awkward silences now?"

"Maybe it's because before, we had a plan. We were working toward a common goal. That first night we were plotting out strategy, last night we were carrying out act one, and tonight act two. It's over now. We don't have anything else to talk about, at least until I come to dinner at your parent's again next week. It's not as if we're friends, or as if we're really dating."

"Maybe we should," he said abruptly.

"Should what?" she asked.

"Really date."

"Why?"

"Why not?" he said.

Shannon clutched her chest and laughed. "Oh, be still my heart. *Why not*, he says. Now those are words to warm a girl's heart. *Why not?* It's sort of like saying, *Do you want a cheeseburger* and having someone answer, *Sure, why not?*"

"Come on, Shannon, that's not what I meant," Nate protested.

She continued talking, as if she hadn't heard him. "I mean, if this is how you sweet talk women, it's clear why you're not married and your mother is pining away after a grandbaby."

"Hey, that's not fair," Nate said. "I sweet talk women just fine."

"Oh, yeah?" Shannon slid closer to him and looked him right in the face. "Say we were dating for real. Pretend I'd invited you in and we were sitting next to each other on my couch. What sweet-nothings would you whisper in my ear?"

His face was a hand's length away from hers. She looked right into his dark brown eyes. No, not quite brown. That was too plain a word to describe the rich color. They were the color of coffee. A perfect mug of Columbian coffee that had been hand roasted to perfection.

"Come on, this isn't fair," Nate protested. "You're putting me on the spot."

"Ha. I rest my case. You, Nathan Calder, are no sweet talker. A man who was used to using smooth words on women wouldn't have any problems coming up with something on the spur of the moment."

"Hey, I can *smooth talk* as well as the next guy," he said.

"Let me just say, ha, again."

"Stop ha-ing me."

"Ha. Ha. Ha. Okay, I'll give you that you talk as smooth as the next guy, but only because guys don't talk smooth at all, unless it's in the movies. And then they only manage it because it was probably a woman writing the script. Men wouldn't know a sweet word if they had a giant thesaurus in front of them."

Nate actually shook a finger at her as he said, "That's a totally sexist thing to say. Men don't need a woman's help to smooth talk a woman."

"That was a rather convoluted sentence, don't you think? And you shook your finger at me like I was some kid that needed scolding."

He dropped his hand on his lap. "I did not."

"Hey, I know a finger-shake when I see one and you definitely shook."

"Shannon, I don't shake fingers."

"Ha. You're a finger-shaking, non-sweet-talking … man."

"There you go, ha-ing me again."

"Finger-shaker."

"Ha-er."

They both paused, faces inches apart and as if on cue, they both burst out laughing.

Nate managed to stop laughing long enough to ask, "Why are we fighting? We've done it. We totally freaked your mom out, and even though my mom loved you yesterday, we'll get her next time. So why are we fighting?"

"*Why not?*" Shannon said with a huge grin.

His smile was a mirror image. "You know, you're a rather annoying woman at times. But then, I think that's a feminine trait. Annoying men."

"Oh, yeah, that's sweet talk if I ever heard it." She batted her eyelids and sighed, "Your melodic prose set my senses aglow."

"You want sweet and smooth? How about this? You're eyes are like …" He paused, and the pause dragged on until it had become silence.

"Oh, you smooth-talking, sweet-worded man, you."

"Hang on. Give me a second to put this together." He took a deep breath and said, "Your eyes are your most striking feature. Oh, when people meet you, they probably think it's your hair—that fire-engine shade is an attention grabber. But anyone around you long knows it's not the hair. You're eyes they … sparkle. They show your every emotion. They grab a hold of a guy, like some sort of charm, and don't let go. I've seen those eyes, your eyes, in my dreams every night since we met."

Shannon laughed, but it sounded forced even to her ears. "Okay, that's enough."

"What? You don't seem amused any longer. Is this making you nervous?" he challenged.

"Why would I be nervous?"

Shannon asked the question because, to be honest, she didn't have a clue why Nate was making her nervous, but he was. Her heart was pounding, her palms were sweating.

Maybe she was sick?

Maybe she was having a heart attack?

It would serve him right if she was. After all, he was the one making her feel this way. Elevating her blood pressure to such a degree that some vessel was bound to give way.

"Maybe you're nervous because I'm looking at your eyes and it makes me wonder what it would be like to kiss you."

"Why would looking at my eyes make you wonder about kissing me? You'd think my lips would do that."

There. She'd told him. Eyes didn't make people think about kissing, but lips did, and looking at Nate's lips, Shannon was pretty sure kissing him wouldn't be a hardship.

"No, just like you'd think your hair should be your most striking feature, but it isn't, it's your eyes, not your lips that makes me thinking about kissing you. Looking in them, I feel as if I've known you forever, and I feel a need to connect with you and that's what makes me want to kiss you. A soft, sweet need to connect."

"Okay," she said, her voice soft and breathy to her own ears. "That was a pretty smooth line."

"It wasn't a line," Nate said, inching closer, closing the slight distance that separated them on the couch. "I'm serious. I want to kiss you."

"But, this is all pretend. It's not as if we're really dating, or anything."

"Who says we couldn't?" he asked.

"Couldn't kiss, or couldn't date?"

"Both."

"Me. I say."

"Why?"

Looking at his lips so close, so tempting, Shannon almost wanted to say *why not* and just kiss him. But she resisted the urge and said, "Listen, I'm not ready to settle down. I like my life. I like sappy movies and not having to shave my legs. I like doing what I want and not worrying about someone else."

"Me, too."

"You like watching sappy movies?" she asked.

"No. Not that part. But I do like my life the way it is. Uncomplicated. That's the beautiful thing about our ... well, whatever it is we could have. We're coming into it knowing what we want. Uncomplicated. If I ask you out and you don't want to go, you can feel free to say no. And vice versa."

"So what you're suggesting is we date, but not really."

"We'd date enough to keep our moms off our backs."

"So, more than just a couple dinners. An on-going casual dating thing? That's what you're suggesting?"

"Yeah," Nate said. "As if we were friends."

"Buddies."

"Pals."

"So," Shannon said, dragging the word out. "If I were to ask if you wanted to watch a movie tonight?"

"Then I'd say I'd much rather kiss you."

"And if I did kiss you?"

"Then I might be tempted to try something more."

"Okay, so let's not take a chance on tempting you," she said. "At least not yet. Let's just watch a movie."

If Nate was annoyed that she was avoiding kissing him he didn't show it. He simply smiled and asked, "What movie?"

"Something old school. Terms of Endearment?"

"No way. That's too sappy for any self-respecting man."

"Steel Magnolias?"

"Even more no way."

"Are you too manly to watch a chick-flick?" she asked with a grin.

"Yeah. Just call me Bull, Ma'am. If it don't got blood and guts, I don't watch it."

"Terminator?"

"Terminator?" That stopped him. "You've got a copy of Terminator in with all those girly films?"

"When you get down to the core of the story, it's a love story."

Shannon had always loved the sweet poignancy of the couple's love in the midst of such horrible odds.

"No way is it a romance," Nate protested.

"When's the last time you watched it?"

"I don't know, but I know Arnold doesn't make chick-flicks."

"Terminator it is, then."

Nate looked at the woman curled in his arms. Shannon had fallen asleep sometime before the end of the movie. He hadn't noticed right away. But gradually, she'd leaned his way, pressing her warm body against his.

Leaning closer and closer.

He'd wrapped an arm around her and had enjoyed the sensation of just holding her.

The credits rolled and he smiled.

She'd been right, Terminator was a romance, though he'd never thought of it that way.

His smiled faded.

What on earth was he doing?

He was holding a sleeping woman in his arms and he felt…almost content.

He'd never even kissed her.

They'd talked about kissing, but hadn't.

Instead they'd simply enjoyed watching a movie together. Shannon had made them popcorn and they sat on the couch like some old married couple watching a movie.

He noticed a stray piece of hair, falling over her eye. It just barely touched her eyelid because her hair was so short.

Normally he liked long hair on women, but on Shannon…well, the short cut worked. It fit her personality. It sort of said, *wild and free-spirited*. But what her hair didn't say was sweet. No, that's where her eyes came in.

Thinking of her eyes made him think about all the stuff he'd said. Sweet, goopy sort of stuff. Where on earth had that come from?

It was well after midnight—well past the time for him to leave—and yet he'd stayed. He didn't know why, but he couldn't bear to wake her. He just wasn't ready to go yet.

The phone rang, jarring him from his musings. Who would be calling her this late at night?

Shannon didn't even move.

Without thinking, Nate grabbed the phone, which was on the end table next to him.

"Hello?" he asked in a hushed whisper.

"Who is this?" a female voice asked.

"Who are you trying to reach?" he countered.

"Shannon. Shannon O'Malley."

"She's sleeping right now. Could I take a message?"

"Is this Bull?"

"Yes," he answered slowly.

Who was this? He was sure it wasn't Mrs. O'Malley. He'd recognize her voice. "With whom am I speaking?"

"*With whom*? That's pretty classy speech for a biker. I'm Shannon's sister, Kate, by the way."

"Ah, Kate. The runaway bride." He kept his voice soft, not wanting to wake Shannon.

"She told you?" Kate asked, surprise evident in her voice, even through a phone-line.

"You'd be surprised how much she's told me," Nate said.

He wasn't sure if he was supposed to carry out his act for Shannon's sister, but he wasn't going to take a chance. If she wanted to explain their relationship and ruse later, that was up to her.

"Well she hasn't mentioned you to me," Kate said.

If he wasn't mistaken, she was annoyed now.

He grinned. "I'm not surprised. We've only known each other a short time."

But it didn't feel like a short time. Other than their short awkward period tonight, Nate felt as if he'd known Shannon a long time. A very long time.

"Tell me about yourself," Kate said. "I got a phone call from my mother, all frantic that Shannon brought you to dinner. You've got Mom totally freaked out, you know. Something's up."

"I don't know what you mean. I'd give the phone to Shannon and let her answer your questions, but she's sleeping. Would you like me to leave her a message?"

"You're answering her phone after midnight because she's sleeping?" Kate asked slowly. "That in itself says a lot. No, don't leave a message. I'll call back tomorrow."

"Great. Good night."

He was ready to hit the disconnect button when he heard Kate say, "Hey, Bull?"

He put the phone back to his ear. "Yes?"

"If you hurt her I'll come after you." Her voice was serious.

Very serious.

"Shannon likes the world to think she's tough, but underneath all her bravado, she's not so tough at all. She's totally soft and vulnerable. I won't have you toying with her."

"Thanks for the warning," he said.

"I mean it."

"I know." He paused and added, "It was nice talking to you, Kate."

"It was interesting talking to you, Bull."

He hung up and glanced at the woman still sleeping in his arms. The video had turned itself off and there was some late-night infomercial about some kitchen appliance on the television.

Nate didn't need to slice or dice anything bad enough to pay twenty-nine, ninety-nine for it.

He should go.

It was late.

And yet, he didn't move. He went back to studying Shannon and wondering what he was doing here, why he was so reluctant to leave.

Sunlight tickled its way beneath Shannon's eyelids, rousing her slowly from whatever she'd been dreaming about.

It was one of those grey, fuzzy sort of dreams that she couldn't quite pinpoint, but she did know that it left her feeling warm. Not in a heat sort of way, but in a comfortable sort of way.

She lay in that halfway state between sleep and wakefulness and realized something wasn't right.

She kept her eyes closed and tried to decide just what was amiss through her sleep-fuzzed brain.

It took a minute to realize what was out of place. That it wasn't a pillow cushioning her head. No, it was something harder, warmer. Something that rose and fell in a rhythmic sort of way. Something like...

A body.

More specifically, her head was cushioned on someone's chest.

Her eyes popped open as the realization struck with full force. She was on the couch in her living room sleeping on Nathan Calder's chest.

How on earth had that happened?

The night came flooding back at full-force.

They'd freaked out her mother, come home, talked about kissing, and a casual dating relationship, then watched *The Terminator*. Only she didn't remember the end of the movie. She remembered sharing popcorn and sitting next to him...

And now she'd spent the night with him.

She grinned.

Oh, that would fry her mom's butt.

She chuckled at the thought. It was enough to shake Nate from his sleep. She felt the change in his breathing pattern and knew he was awake before his eyes even opened.

"Good morning," she said brightly.

He sat up and pulled back, distancing himself from her. "Shannon, I'm so sorry. I meant to get up and go right after the movie, but you were sleeping so peacefully, then your sister called—"

"My sister? Kate called here?"

"And we talked for a while, then I was going to go, but I sat a moment and next thing I knew…well, this was the next thing I knew. I'm sorry."

"Nate, it's okay."

"No, it isn't. I've…" he paused, obviously searching for the word. "Imposed. Yeah, imposed. I didn't mean to."

"Nate, really it's fine." She didn't want to tell him that she sort of enjoyed waking up next to him. That she liked the warmth of his body. She could tell him there was something rather comfortable about snuggling next to him. She could, but she wouldn't.

She simply repeated, "It's okay."

"But—"

"No harm, no foul. I mean, it's not as if you compromised my virtue." She didn't add that compromising with Nate was starting to look sort of appealing.

She sat up and ran her fingers through her hair, knowing that appealing wasn't quite the word she'd use to describe her morning look.

"I guess you're right," he said slowly. "After all, I didn't even kiss you, so your virtue is still very much intact."

"There you go. See, no problem. Tell you what, if you give me a couple minutes to grab a shower, I'll even play hostess and offer you breakfast."

"Yeah?" he asked with a grin.

"Yeah."

"Does your hospitality extend to letting me grab a shower as well?"

"I'm pretty sure that the book on etiquette my mother gave me when I turned sixteen would demand that I—"

"Offer a guest a shower?" he filled in.

"Yeah."

Nate laughed. "You're nuts. Go get your shower and I'll make myself at home. I'll even make the coffee since you're making the breakfast."

"Oh, you are a true gentleman, Bull."

"Yeah, Roxy, I try."

Shannon scampered off to get her shower and Nate watched her disappear down the hall.

He'd just spent his first night with her.

And he realized he didn't want it to be the last night they spent together. Not that he was looking for anything permanent, nothing like his mother envisioned. But more nights with Shannon … that he could handle.

Nate poked around in her kitchen, locating the coffee and the filters in the cupboard over the coffee maker. It was a small kitchen, bright, without all the loud colors his mother favored. No, this was softer with a lot of white's and pale yellows.

It suited Shannon.

He'd just got the coffee ready and had pushed the button to start it when he heard the front door open.

"Shannon?" a voice called.

A voice Nate recognized immediately.

Well, Shannon wanted her mother to believe they were an item, and it appeared she was going to get that wish answered in spades.

He walked out of the kitchen into the living room where a very annoyed looking Mrs. O'Malley stood.

"I saw your motorcycle in the drive," she said, disapproval evident in her voice.

"Yeah. I didn't plan on staying the night or I'd've put it in the garage. I don't like letting my baby stay outside all night."

Last night Mrs. O'Malley had been knocked off guard, but she'd had time to regroup. Her stance would do a three-star general proud. Her tone left no doubt that she was back in control. "Where is my daughter?"

"In the shower. I was just making coffee. Could I offer you a cup?"

"No. I'm on my way to Mass and stopped to see if Shannon wanted to join me."

"Want me to go ask her?" he asked, smiling as if he didn't have a clue why she'd take offense at the question.

Mrs. O'Malley sputtered a moment, looking as if she'd swallowed a cow whole. "I don't think so. Tell her I'll call her later."

"Sure thing."

"And Bull?" Mrs. O'Malley said, moving a few steps closer.

"Yes, ma'am?"

"If you hurt her, you'll answer to me."

Some of the humor left the situation. Nate raked a hand through his hair. "You're the second O'Malley to tell me that in less than a day's time. What is it that makes you all think Shannon couldn't take care of me herself if I hurt her?"

Her sister and mother might not think so, but Nate suspected Shannon was more than capable of standing up for herself. From what he could see, all the O'Malley women were formidable.

"Shannon's too soft-hearted for her own good," her mother said. "She believes in fairytales. I think that's why she enjoyed planning her sister's wedding so much. But I know that romance isn't enough. That people need more than a good shot of lust to make a relationship work. I don't think the two of you could possibly have that much in common. Odds are, this will end badly. I don't want her hurt."

"And yet, you're willing to see her married off just to win a bet," Nate said gently.

Mrs. O'Malley heaved a sigh and shook her head. "No. I want to see her married off because Shannon is the type of person who's meant to be married. She needs someone to love, someone who will in turn love her to distraction. This bet... well, it simply presented an excuse to introduce her around."

"Someone to take care of her, you mean?"

"I say what I mean, young man," Mrs. O'Malley's voice was once again sharp and in command. "I raised both of my daughters to be able to take care of themselves, but I also think life is more meaningful if you share it with someone."

She paused a moment and added, "Do you think you're the man Shannon should be sharing her life with?"

"Maybe. Maybe not. But I know that none of the guys you've set her up with are him," Nate said.

"So do I."

Her admission surprised him. "And yet, you continued to set her up."

"In hopes that the next man would be the right man. The one she's been waiting for."

"And you're sure I'm not *him*?" he asked.

"As sure as I can be. Shannon needs an ordinary man. Someone who will come home every night after work. She needs the simple things, trading stories about their days, eating a quiet meal together. Something as simple as watching a movie together. Someone with common interests. I don't think that's you."

"Maybe you're right," Nate said. "Maybe I'm not her Mr. Right, but I am her Mr. Right-now, so I'll thank you to forget about setting her up with anyone else for a while."

"Fine," Mrs. O'Malley said with a short nod. "Tell her I'll talk to her later."

"Sure."

She started toward the door, then abruptly turned around. "And Bull, remember what I said."

"Don't worry, I don't intend to hurt her."

Mrs. O'Malley turned and left, shutting the front door with a soft thud.

Nate went back to the kitchen and poured a cup of coffee for himself as he pondered his confrontation with Shannon's mom.

Mrs. O'Malley was right. From the little Nate knew about her, Shannon was special. He'd know it that first night in Mick's bar. And now, having spent time with her, he was even more convinced.

He thought—

"Hey, a man who makes me coffee in the morning, that's my kind of man," Shannon said, as she came into the kitchen, her hair still wet. She was wearing jeans and a t-shirt. Her feet were bare. She didn't have a spec of make-up on.

She looked as far removed from Roxy as a woman could.

And yet, this look was ever so much sexier.

He forced himself not to think about how much sexier as he handed her a mug of coffee.

"I believe you said something about breakfast," he reminded her.

She grinned. "Sure did."

"So what are you making me?" he asked.

"Nothing. We're going to get on your motorcycle, and drive down the street to Perkins. There, I plan to order a huge stack of pancakes, and drown them in syrup. How about you?"

"So, I made the coffee, and you're allowing me to take you to Perkins?"

"Hey, it's my treat."

"I wanted to try your cooking," he said. "After growing up with my mother, well, let's just say, I like to know how a woman cooks right up front."

"In this case, you don't."

"That bad?" he asked.

"Uh, you know your mom's roast the other night? That looked good in comparison."

"Thanks for the warning then. Perkins it is."

"I thought you might see it that way," she said with a laugh.

"Do you mind if I get that shower before we go?"

"Help yourself."

"Thanks."

"And Nate?" she called as he started toward the bathroom.

"Yeah?"

"I'm glad you spent the night."

"Me, too," he said, then turned and hurried down the hall. He liked being here with Shannon, liked holding her last night.

He just plain liked her.

And he didn't have a clue what to do about it.

CHAPTER SIX

Shannon held the phone away from her ear and looked at it, as if it could provide some answers.

She put it back to her ear, and said, "The dress?"

"Yes. I need that dress back. When you get married, you'll have to find your own dress. I've decided Mary Kathryn's—"

"Kate," Shannon corrected automatically.

"Kate's dress doesn't suit you."

She'd won.

Her mother might be saying the dress doesn't suit, but what she meant was that *Bull* didn't suit.

Her mom was done trying to marry Shannon off to just any man.

Shannon was free and clear.

Why wasn't she feeling elated?

"Honey, I want you to find the right man when the time's right. You don't have to rush anything."

"What about the bet?"

"Don't you worry about that. I love you and just want you to be happy."

"Mom," Shannon said. She sniffed.

A moment.

She'd just had *a moment* with her mother.

"Mom," she said again.

Brigit O'Malley was not one for big demonstrations. "Get that dress ready. I'll pick it up later."

"About Bull," Shannon said, ready to confess all, to tell her mother her nefarious plan.

"Not one more word. This was a good conversation and I'll not have it ruined by fighting about your boyfriend. I'll stop by later this week and pick up the dress," she said, hanging up abruptly.

Shannon was victorious.

Her mom was off her back.

She could let the hair on her legs grow so long she would be able to braid it.

She could go on a weeklong chick-flick-fest.

There was a world of opportunities in front of her.

But what she really wanted to do was call Nate and share her victory.

Truth be told, she'd wanted to call him after he dropped her off that day. She thought about calling to thank him for breakfast. Maybe to see how the ride home had gone.

Had he stalled the motorcycle?

But she didn't call. Didn't want him to think she was reading more into their *casual* relationship than he was.

She didn't call and hoped he would.

He didn't.

He didn't call Monday either.

Neither did she.

As much as she wanted to call him, she just couldn't.

She must have picked up the phone a dozen times, but always slammed it back down.

She wasn't sure why it was so hard to call him. She had the perfect excuse, to share the news about her mom. But she didn't call, and neither did he.

Wednesday was a repeat performance. Look at the phone. Think about calling. Even go so far as to pick up the phone. Set it back down. Don't call.

Thursday she didn't pick up the phone at all. Oh she thought about it, but since he hadn't called her, she wasn't about to call him.

She realized just how juvenile she was behaving, but didn't seem to be able to stop herself. Something about Nate made her feel as if she was back in high school, giggling with girlfriends over boys.

Friday she woke up with a light heart. She and Nate were having dinner at his mom's again tonight. She'd see him after school.

She practically danced through the day. Even Robbie Pembrooke, a student who could try the patience of a saint, couldn't faze her happiness.

Of course, she did inform him that graffiti didn't qualify as an art project … at least not in her class. She made him stay after school to clean his *project* off the side of the school and write a letter of apology to Mrs. Appleton, who, to the best of Shannon's knowledge, did not, nor ever had, had drinking problem.

Although if the rumor about the rest of the Pembrooke clan was true, by the time the four children made it through the school the entire staff just might be falling down drunks.

No, even Robbie Pembrooke couldn't phase her good mood.

Shannon noticed that Robbie had stopped scrubbing and was simply standing in front of the wall.

"Robbie," Shannon hollered.

He turned and said, "My arm's killing me," with that teenaged whine that would one day grow into a fine man-whine.

"Tough," she said.

The boy turned back and started scrubbing again. And Shannon smiled.

"You look awfully happy," her friend, Patricia said, as she took a seat next to Shannon on the bench. "So, what's up?"

"Maybe it's just a happy sort of day. It is Friday, after all."

Patricia shook her head. "I know a Friday-smile when I see one, and this is something more."

"Well, it just so happens I have a date."

She didn't admit that it wasn't exactly a date.

"Oooh, do tell. Does it involve candlelight and a new outfit?"

"Yes, to the new outfit." Shannon had gone shopping yesterday and was pretty sure her outfit was going to scandalize Nathan's mom.

Yes, one look at those pants and Mrs. Calder was going to be so scandalized she'd beg Nate to stop dating *Roxy*.

The thought should have made her feel victorious, but instead, she felt a bit letdown.

"Yes, new clothes, but not candlelight. Just a quiet dinner. Not much to tell. Just me, on a date."

"That's it?" Patricia asked, sounding a bit skeptical.

"Yep."

"Hmm," Patricia said, studying her.

"Robbie, you missed a spot," Shannon called, ignoring Patricia's scrutiny. She smiled as Robbie grumbled, not because he grumbled, but because she was going to see Nate in just a few hours.

"So, how are the kids?" she asked. And even as she listened to Patricia talk about her kids, she couldn't help but smile.

She'd see Nate tonight.

"Oh, Shannon, dear, I'm so sorry," Mrs. Calder said as they entered the house that evening.

Shannon didn't have to ask just what it was Mrs. Calder was sorry for. There was a distinct smell of burnt—well, she wasn't sure just what was burnt, but whatever it had been, it was charcoal now.

"I made the most lovely veal for dinner—"

Ah, veal, that's what it was.

"—but there must be something wrong with my oven."

"Or with your cooking," Nate muttered low enough so that only Shannon caught it.

She stifled the laughter that bubbled just below the surface. She'd felt giddy since Nate showed up on her doorstep. He was wearing jeans and a polo shirt... looking positively good wonderful.

"That's okay, Mrs. Calder," she assured his mom. "Really."

"No, dear, I promised you dinner and you're getting dinner. Why, I don't imagine you get to eat right at the club you work at. I think they're more interested in drinking than good food. So, let's go."

"Go?" Shannon echoed, realizing that this burnt meal could be a problem.

A big problem.

"We're going out to eat." Mrs. Calder started to gather her purse.

"But..." Shannon looked down at tonight's exotic-dancer outfit.

Tight pseudo-leather—pleather—pants, a bright red blouse and stiletto black heels. Add to that, she'd slicked her hair back with goop and piled on the make-up. She didn't want to go out in public looking like this.

"But..." she stammered.

Nate hadn't said a word. She elbowed him hard and looked from him to her outfit, then back at him. She saw the dawning of understanding on his face.

"Mom, really, that's okay," he said in a rush. "We'll come back to dinner tomorrow, and you can try again."

"Ah, son, I know you love my cooking."

Nate shot Shannon a look and she knew exactly what he was thinking... his mom was the worst cook alive.

"But, really darling," Mrs. Calder continued. "I enjoy a night off now and then as well. So, let's go."

"Pizza," Nate said. "Let's just order in pizza."

"Now, will you two stop fighting? We're eating out. Paul," she hollered.

Shannon didn't have to be her child to realize that was that. Mrs. Calder wasn't going to be dissuaded.

Mr. Calder ambled into the foyer. "Shannon. How nice to see you again. I assume you heard about our change of plans."

Nate nodded. "Where do you want us to meet you?"

"I was hoping we could all ride together," his mom said.

"You don't like my motorcycle," Nate accused.

"It's not that..." his mom started, then shrugged. "Okay, it is that. I don't like it. And if you were to crash on the way out to dinner, I'd never get over the guilt. You'd be maimed because I can't cook. You don't want to put your mother through something like that, do you? After all, you're the only child I could have and the suffering I went through to get you... why, you couldn't willingly subject me to any more, could you?"

"Mom, that's ridiculous. I'm a grown man and—"

"We'd love to ride with you, Mrs. Calder," Shannon interrupted.

"Thank you, dear, for understanding."

"No problem."

His parents walked out the door and toward the Calder's blue sedan.

Nate hung back and held Shannon back as well. "Why did you do that?" he whispered.

"Because she worries about you. There's nothing wrong with that."

"Not when it's my mom doing the worrying," he said, obviously put out. "But when it's your mom, then it's another story."

"My mom doesn't worry. She bosses. There's a difference," Shannon said.

"She bosses you around because she's worried about you," Nate countered.

"Since when did you become and expert on my mother?"

"Let's just say that maybe I have a bit more objective insights than you do."

"Let's not and have you explain."

"Just leave it alone, Shannon."

"Are you two coming," Nate's mom called from the car. She paused and said, "Is something wrong?"

"No, of course not," Shannon said as she shook her arm free of Nate and walked toward the car.

"Good," she said with a smile. "Then we're off."

Nate poked at his dinner salad as he listened to Shannon and his mother chatter away happily.

Shannon was making a mess of things again. His mother seemed to enjoy her as much tonight as she had last week. At the rate Shannon was going, he was going to be married off and the father of four.

Somehow the thought didn't send the familiar jolt of terror down his spine. Not that he was thinking of marrying

Shannon. If he had to get married, she'd be number one on his list.

And thinking he'd even have a list of women he'd marry totally freaked him out and he kicked her leg under the table and shot her a get-on-with-it-already look.

He knew she caught the gist of his meaning because she winked at him and said, "I've been thinking about changing jobs."

"Really, dear, that would be wonderful. Not that what you do for a living affects our opinion of you. After all, you're such a sweet and caring young lady."

"Why, thank you, Mrs. Calder." Shannon smiled sweetly at the praise.

Of course, the loud red color she'd painted on her lips should have made smiling sweetly very difficult, but Shannon pulled it off.

"So what are you thinking about doing?" his mom asked.

"I'm going to—"

"Shannon, it is you," someone interrupted her.

Nate looked up and saw a petite brunette and a tall skinny man standing next to their table.

"Patricia?" Shannon said weakly. She glanced down and blushed.

Nate realized that she obviously knew the couple, and it was just as obvious that she was embarrassed to be caught in her Roxy get-up.

"What are you two doing here? And where are the kids?" Shannon asked.

"Kyle was sweet enough to invite me to dinner and I left the kids with a sitter. Are you going to introduce us?" Patricia asked.

Shannon smiled, and Nate suspected he was the only one who noticed how forced it was.

"Patricia Leonard and Kyle Bruno, this is Nate Calder and his parents, Paul and Judy."

"These are your friends from work, dear?" Mrs. Calder asked.

Nate suddenly realized that these were the friends she'd based her little strip-club stories on and suppressed a groan.

Their plans were about to tank all because his mother was a lousy cook.

He knew what he was getting her for Christmas…cooking lessons. She didn't have to be a cordon bleu chef, but man, you'd think at her age she could broil a hunk of meat without charbroiling it and ruining all his plans in the process.

He'd be the first man in history forced to walk down the aisle because of a burnt meal.

"Why, Shannon," his mother said, "you didn't tell us Candy here was dating Bruno. That's wonderful."

"Candy?" Patricia asked.

"She prefers to be called Patricia," Shannon corrected.

This time Nate didn't try to suppress his groan. No, he let it out, knowing that if his mother noticed it would be the least of their worries.

Shannon had told his mom that Patricia stripped under the name Candy and of course his mom—the woman who could forget about dinner until the smoke alarms went off—didn't forget little things like Shannon's fictional account of her fictional job at the fictional strip club using her real colleagues fictional stripping name.

"How come you didn't tell me you two were dating," Shannon said.

Nate could tell she was trying to head off further questions by her friends, but he could have told her, the way his luck was going, it wasn't going to work.

"We didn't really want anyone to know," Patricia said. "It's all so new and you know how it is at work. Everyone knows everyone's business."

"Tell me about it," Shannon muttered.

Nate could tell she was thinking about everyone at school knowing this particular business on Monday.

It occurred to him that reading her was getting easier and easier, and he wasn't quite sure how he felt about that.

"I suppose people in your line of work tend to band together," his mother said. "I mean, it's wonderful to have friends who understand what you do and why. People who don't judge you," his mom said.

"Oh, you're so right," Patricia said. "So many people just hear the bad stuff, how tough it can be. They don't understand that there are good things involved with the job. That the good things far outweigh the bad."

"Shannon was just telling us about it the other night. Would you like to join us?" his mom said. "I'd love to have a chance to get to know Shannon's friends better now that she and Nate are so close."

"Sure. We'd love to," Patricia, aka Candy, said as she pulled up a chair from a neighboring table. "So, Nate, how long have you and Shannon been seeing each other?"

"A while," he said as noncommittally as he could manage. He turned to Kyle, aka Bruno the Bouncer. "How 'bout those Pirates?"

"Yeah. How 'bout them?" Kyle countered. "I think they can go all the way this year." He turned to Nate's dad and said, "You?"

"An Indian fan through and through."

Nate worked at keeping the conversation turned to sports. He figured if they were talking balls and strikes loud enough his mom couldn't start to cross-examine Shannon's friend about *work*.

"Patricia..." his mom said.

"And what about the Otters still being in the play-offs?" Nate said, hoping to out-talk his mom. He should have known it wouldn't work. "It's so great to still have hockey games so far into the spring."

His mom shot him an evil glare and continued, "So, how long have you worked at... well, with Shannon?"

"Oh, it must be three years now, right Shannon?" Patricia said.

"Yeah," she answered, sounding as morose as he felt.

"I've been to all the home games," Nate said. "I play amateur hockey with some friends."

"Me, too," said Kyle. "A bunch of us at work got together and formed a team. We've got games through July. I love baseball, but hockey, now that's a tough sport."

Nate's mom picked right up on that. "The people you... work with are on a hockey team?"

"Co-ed. It's just for fun. Work can be so stressful, there are just so many demands on us. We need somewhere to unwind. And there's no better way to de-stress than skating around an ice rink hitting pucks."

"I imagine you do need an outlet given the circumstances," his mom said. "It's good that all the women at work have you to look after them."

Kyle grinned at Patricia. "I look after some a little more closely than others."

"Well, I'm sure you're a gentleman. Shannon told me that you've been her hero on more than one occasion."

"Oh, yeah. There was that time the Pembrooke clan got together and...

Chapter Seven

"Well, now, that was an interesting night," Nate said as they walked up to Shannon's porch.

Interesting was going to be the discussion in the teacher's room on Monday. Trying to explain what happened ... yeah, that would be interesting.

For the life of her, Shannon couldn't think of a way to explain her outfit.

Somehow they'd made it through the meal without having Nate's mom see through their deception, but it had been a near thing more than once. Thank goodness for the Erie Otters being in the play-offs. The guys had kept that conversation going for quite a while.

"Interesting," Shannon repeated. "Yeah, you can say that again."

She stood, staring out at the streetlights wondering if she could bribe Patricia and Kyle into silence.

Oh, her date was going to be all over the faculty room on Monday, she just knew it.

"That was ..." Nate left the sentence hang, smiling as he stood next to her.

"Funny, Calder. Real funny. Let's see how funny you'd think it was if some of your customers from the pharmacy saw you all bikered up."

His smile faded abruptly and he laid a hand lightly on her shoulder. It was meant to be comforting. "You're really upset," he said, softly.

She nodded.

"Yes, I am."

"Hey, I'm sorry."

She shrugged. "It wasn't your fault."

"I should have refused to go out with my mom. I just don't know how to tell her no sometimes."

"Tell me about it. It's not your fault I'm in this absurd situation. It's my mother's. Your not being able to say no to a dinner is far more understandable than my not being able to say no to a wedding."

"I know you don't want to hear this right now," Nate said slowly, "but I have to confess, I'm sort of grateful to your mom."

"Grateful?" Of all the things she'd expect to hear him say, that wasn't one.

"Grateful?" she repeated.

"Yeah. I mean, if your mom hadn't come up with that bet and started throwing you at men, you wouldn't have ended up at Mick's. If you hadn't ended up at Mick's, then I wouldn't have met you. If I hadn't met you I wouldn't be standing here on your porch, with a full moon blazing over-head, thinking about doing this—"

There was no time to think, no time to prepare, though even if there had been, Shannon would have been defense-less as Nate stopped talking and moved toward her. He turned her gently until she was facing him and then low-ered his lips to hers.

She could have turned her head.

She could have backed away.

Instead, she met the kiss.

Any thoughts of ruined reputations, or overbearing mothers were immediately lost in the sensation of kissing Nate.

The smell of him, the taste of him, the firmness of his lips, the warmth of his body pressed to hers. Shannon was swimming in a sea of sensations—drowning in them.

The kiss eased and slowly, their lips parted, but neither of them released their hold on the other.

"Wow," Nate said as he released his breath.

Shannon laughed. "Oh so eloquent, as always, Mr. Calder."

"How's this for eloquent... I want you. Not just some kiss on your porch, but all of you. I want to take you inside, into your room and—"

"Nate," she said, interrupting his description because it so well matched her own thoughts... her own desires. "I don't know. I don't want to take our charade, our partnership, and try to turn it into something that it's not. What we have is fiction. Even our casual dating agreement isn't a real relationship."

"I'm not suggesting marriage. I'm suggesting that this could be good. Very good. I think over the last two weeks we've developed something more than fiction... we've become friends. We both understand that we're not ready for a lifelong commitment. Why can't that friendship extend to what we both so obviously want?"

"Nate, I've come to value your friendship. I know we haven't known each other long, but you mean something to me. Something I'm not willing to lose. Do you really think we could be intimate and still just be friends?"

"Why not? A friendship that extends into the bedroom." He paused. "Bedroom buddies."

"*Why not?*" she repeated with a laugh. "Yes, you are eloquent."

"You want something more eloquent? How about this." He paused a moment, then said, "I haven't been able to get you out of my head since that first night at Mick's. I like being with you. I like laughing with you. I liked holding you in my arms while you slept last week. Hell, I didn't even mind watching a chick-flick with you."

"You said Terminator wasn't a chick flick," she pointed out with a laugh.

"I lied. You were right. It's a romance."

"And this? What will this thing between us be, Nate?"

"We're friends. Friends who want to be with one another."

"And that will be enough?" She was asking the question of Nate, but really, it was meant for herself.

Could it be enough to just be intimate friends with Nate?

What had he said—bedroom buddies. Friends who occasionally slept together, but had no real commitment?

Could that work?

She didn't know the answer.

"It could be enough, I think. At least for me," he said. "What about for you?"

"I don't know the answer to that. I'll confess, I've had boyfriends in the past, but no one I've wanted the way I want you. No one I felt this sense of friendship... this sense of connection with."

"Is that enough?" he asked softly as he pulled her close, tighter within the shelter of his arms.

"For now," she said, nodding as she answered her own question. "Yes. It can be enough for now."

Decision made, she didn't want to think or analyze any more. She just wanted him—immediately, if not sooner.

She fumbled through her purse for her keys. Two tries later, she couldn't contain the tremor in her hand long enough to get the key into the hole.

"Let me," Nate said.

He unlocked the door and swept her inside, slamming the door behind him. He dropped the keys, and they landed on the tile with a clank.

"I—"

"Shh. We're not talking. We're ..."

Without releasing his hold on her, they started up the stairs.

Shannon was just getting the hang of walking back-wards and kissing when she thwacked to an abrupt halt, her back pressed against her bedroom door, her front pressed against Nate. She reached behind her back fumbled with the knob and they both practically fell into the room as the door swung inward.

They stood at the end of her bed and she wrapped her arms around his neck.

Shannon pulled back and tried to catch her breath, but Nate didn't seem to want to oblige. His hands were tug-ging at her shirt, pulling it up and off. And suddenly she was helping him, needing to remove any barriers between them. As he slid off his own shirt, she unbuttoned her pants and tugged downward.

They didn't budge.

Not even an inch.

She tried again. But, unfortunately, pleather seemed to have a lot of the same characteristics as leather. It didn't slide well on hot, sticky skin.

And even more unfortunate, Shannon was definitely hot ... and not because of the temperature, but because of the man standing next to her, watching as she tugged at the waistband of the pants. The fabric moved a millimeter toward her feet and then stuck again, as if superglued.

"Problems?" Nate asked, tossing his shirt on the floor.

She stared at his naked chest. It was a sight to behold. Firm, without being overworked. He looked like a man who was active enough, without being obsessed by his body.

"Shannon?" he said, reaching for the snap on his jeans.

"Yes?" she said, her voice practically a whisper.

She knew he was asking her something, but she was mesmerized by the sight of him and had lost track of what she'd been doing and what he was asking. She reached out and grazed a line down his chest with the tip of her finger.

"Shannon, you stopped. What's wrong?"

Stopped? Her mind was fuzzy. She felt almost drunk on the sight of him.

"Stopped?" she echoed.

"Stopped undressing."

"I, uh…" What were they talking about? She didn't have a clue. She stood, frozen to the spot, watching every movement Nate made.

"Shannon-me-love," he crooned, his face lowered and just a breath away from her own.

His lips grazed hers again.

Her chest pressed to his, her heartbeat melded with his.

Thump, thump.

Thump, thump.

It was as if there was no separation between them. They were one.

One breath.

One heartbeat.

"Here, let me help," he said as his hands hooked onto her waistband and tugged.

The pants didn't move.

Suddenly she remembered what she'd been doing when he removed his shirt.

She remembered the fact that she was stuck in her pants.

Nate's lips left hers and he looked down, studying the problem.

"Uh?"

"They're fake leather," she said as she joined his tugging. "They say it's like leather, but maybe they should say it's like a chastity belt. Parents all over the world would buy pseudo-leather pants for their daughters."

They both tugged and the pants slipped down another fraction of a millimeter.

"Maybe if you sat down on the bed and I pulled," Nate said.

Shannon nodded. She was starting to feel a bit claustrophobic about being stuck in her pants. What if they couldn't get them off?

She sat on the edge of the bed and gripped the footboard.

Nate pulled.

Hard.

She was glad she'd held on, because her pants didn't move at all, but her body practically flew off the bed, suspended between the footboard and Nate's grip on her pant-legs she hung like a suspension bridge.

Nate let her settle back down onto the mattress and Shannon could have sworn she heard a chuckle, but when she checked he looked serious.

"I don't think this is working," she said. "I should have taken them off before I got so..."

"Hot?" he supplied, unable to continue his fake-seriousness he was grinning.

Leave it to a man to find the idea that he'd got her so worked up that she was stuck in her pants a compliment.

"It is warm out tonight."

"I don't think that's why you're all hot," he said. "No, I don't think it has a thing to do with the weather."

"You're enjoying this." He reached for her again, and she moved back. "Let me think a minute."

"Do you have any powder?" he asked.

"Powder?"

"Maybe if we shake a little into your pants it will help."

"You want to powder my pants?" She giggled. "Ah, Bull, you are a kinky man."

"Ah, but you love it, Roxy."

They both burst out laughing, full, deep, catch-your-breath-when-you-were-done sort of laughter.

When she could breathe again, she said, "You know, this has never happened before."

"Getting stuck in your pants?" He gave the waistband another little tug, but it didn't move at all.

"No. This. Laughing like this when I'm…" she paused, looking for the right word.

He just grinned and quirked an eyebrow.

They both burst out laughing again.

Maybe it was nerves, or maybe, just maybe there was something special about her relationship with Nate. Something more than just friendship. Something that warranted reflection.

But she'd reflect tomorrow. Right now, she just wanted to get her pants off.

She found a bottle of powder from her vanity and sprinkled some liberally into her pants, reaching down the legs and rubbing it as far down as she could.

Nate sat on the edge of the bed, watching her every move. "Want help?"

"If you help I'm bound to get hotter, which will ultimately defeat the purpose. Stay there."

"Are you sure?" he asked. The laughter had died from his voice. Now she heard something else, something thick and hot.

"Yes, I'm sure."

"So, basically, you want me to stay over here and watch you ... strip."

"Yeah. Remember, no touching."

"Your boss has rules, right, Roxy?" he asked. There was humor in the question, but underneath that was desire.

"Right, my boss has rules."

He leaned back on his elbows and watched. "Ah, Roxy, I'm a lucky man."

"Don't forget it, Bull."

She worked the powder down as far as she could, and pulled again. The pants moved. Slowly, bit by bit, she eased them over her hips. Once clear, they came off.

Free at last.

"Hey, Roxy, I like the undies."

Shannon blushed, knowing he was looking at her thong underwear. "I bought them to go with the outfit. They made me feel sexier."

He pulled her toward the bed. "I think you should wear them all the time."

"Really?" she asked, her voice a whisper.

"Really. Thinking of you in your powder blue oxford shirt, jeans and sneakers, so proper on the outside, but knowing you have these on underneath, and that I'm the only one who knows about them ... I think I'd like it."

She was sitting next to him, and his hands were moving all over her, as if he was trying to memorize every inch of her body.

"Move a bit closer," he murmured, pulling her next to him, so that their thighs touched.

She was falling back under his spell... falling hard. "I don't know, Bull. Mama says bikers are dangerous," she murmured.

"Yeah we are. Live on the wild side."

"Now, where were we?" he asked.

CHAPTER EIGHT

Shannon woke up to the sensation of warmth and weight. It took a moment for her sleep-fogged mind to register just what that meant.

Somebody was in her bed.

More specifically, Nathan, aka Bull, Calder was next to her, hogging the covers.

Even more specifically... she liked it.

This was the second time she'd woken up next to him.

She smiled as she inched closer to him until the length of him was pressed against her back. He shifted in his sleep, wrapping his arms around her.

She'd slept with Nate, both figuratively and literally.

The thought kept chasing itself around in her brain. It was easier to acknowledge the sleeping part than the part that came before they slept.

This was just a friendship that extended to the bedroom.

Which made it hard to classify what they did as *making love*, but making love is exactly how it felt to Shannon even if she couldn't call it that. She wasn't sure what to call it.

Sex sounded too raw and hard.

She thought of the terms she'd overheard kids at school use. Most sounded worse than sex.

Then she hit on *boinking* and smiled. It sounded light and fun, sort of like what they'd done.

If what they'd done wasn't making love, then it was by its very definition light.

She remembered how they'd laugh about the pleather pants incident. She'd never laughed in the middle of … boinking.

Light and fun.

She'd boinked Nathan Calder.

He wasn't her boyfriend. He was a friend who was male. A partner.

And so they weren't lovers and they were no longer just friend and allies.

They were … boink-buddies.

She laughed.

"What's so funny?"

She turned and looked at the man next to her.

"Sorry. I didn't mean to wake you."

"You didn't," he assured her. "I've been awake for a while now."

"Why didn't you get up?"

"I was just enjoying the scenery."

"Scenery?" She didn't have a window in the room you could see from her bed. Suddenly his meaning occurred to her. "Oh."

He grinned. "So, why were you laughing?"

"I was just trying to define …" she hesitated, "Well, this. What we have between us."

He shifted slightly, reminding Shannon she was naked in bed with him.

"And did you?" he asked, his voice low and … well, sexy.

Shannon didn't feel sexy. She felt naked and more than a little rumpled.

"Did you, Shannon-me-love?"

"Did I what?" she asked, unsure what they'd been talking about, but totally sure that whatever it was, wasn't nearly as enthralling as the naked man next to her.

"Did you decide how to define us?" he asked.

"Yep. You said bedroom buddies, but I have a much better term."

"Are you going to tell me?" He reached out and toyed with her hair.

This was definitely better than hairy legs and chick-flicks.

"Shannon?" he murmured. "What's your new term for us?"

She grinned. "Boink-buddies."

"What?" he asked.

"Well, I couldn't quite define us as lovers."

"Why not?"

She'd expected to hear laughter in his voice when she'd revealed her term for their relationship. But that didn't sound like humor, but more like annoyance. She shifted slightly, putting space between them.

"Why wouldn't you define us as lovers?" he pressed.

"Because we're not. You don't love me. I don't love you. We like each other. We're partners. Friends. A friendship that extends to the bedroom. Remember?"

Nate remembered all right. After all, he'd been the one spouting that nonsense last night. And last night it had sounded perfectly logical and completely desirable to just be bedroom buddies.

But this morning?

He didn't want logic.

He didn't want to be just friends who slept together.

And he didn't want what he'd done with Shannon reduced to such a frivolous term as boink-buddies.

What they'd done had been … magic. He winced at the term. It sounded way too sentimental for him to be using, but it was accurate.

Magic.

What they'd done together had been so much more than anything he'd ever experienced, and Shannon was doing her best to minimize it.

"Nate, what's wrong?" she asked softly.

"Nothing," he said, though he knew it for the lie it was. There was something more than just *boinking* between him and Shannon.

Making love?

It certainly sounded more accurate than boinking.

Normally using a phrase like *making love* would be what made him grimace. But not this time. Not with Shannon.

Yet, he didn't point the fact out to her. Why? Because using the term out loud would give it a power he wasn't sure he was willing to give.

She moved further away from him.

"I think I'm going to grab a shower, if you don't mind," she said. "Obviously you're not a morning person."

"What makes you say that?" he asked.

He heard the sharpness in his voice, but was annoyed enough that he didn't try and temper it.

"You're grumpy and quiet. I'll just let you wake up while I get dressed."

"Fine."

She wrapped the top blanket around her, and took it with her as she got out of the bed. He wasn't going to even get to enjoy the view.

Great.

What had looked like it might be a promising morning suddenly looked as if it couldn't get any worse.

Shannon had her shower, then headed to the kitchen. The atmosphere was oppressing.

Nate was still quiet and Shannon wasn't sure if it was indeed just a morning mood. He seemed put out about something.

Maybe he regretted what they'd done.

Maybe he thought she'd suddenly start placing all kinds of girl-friend demands on him. Well, she thought as she dug around in the cupboard for a coffee filter, she wasn't about to do that.

She didn't want a significant other any more than he did.

They were friendly allies and boink-buddies, nothing more, nothing less. That didn't give either of them any rights to make demands.

Actually, a demand-less relationship was what they'd planned, so if that's why he was mad, well he could just get over himself.

Granted, last night was the best boinking she'd ever had.

Having a man who could make her laugh even as he made her quiver with desire... well, that was rare and special. A man like that was to be treasured.

But treasuring didn't mean owning.

"Do you want anything to go with the coffee?" Shannon asked the silent, grumpy man sitting at her counter.

"You can't cook, remember?"

"I can make a bowl of cold cereal," she assured him.

Okay, so cooking wasn't her forte, but it wasn't as if she couldn't pour some milk.

"Are you sure? I—"

The doorbell interrupted him.

After the way the morning started, Shannon fig-ured things couldn't get worse ... then the doorbell rang again.

"Shannon? Open up. It's your mother."

Things had just gone from worse to *worse-r.*

"Oh, rats." She stayed in the kitchen, hiding in case her mother peeked through the door's small window. "Do you think I can wait her out?"

"Shannon, I know you're in there," her mother called.

"Nope. I think she knows you're here. And since my Harley's out front, I'm betting she knows I'm here as well," Nate—ever-the-optimist—said.

"Rats."

"Want me to get it?" he offered.

If she wasn't still annoyed with his less than pleasant mood this morning, she might sigh and think something like, *my hero.* But she was annoyed.

He regretted last night and that was what accounted for his attitude.

Well, fine. Let him regret it.

It wasn't as if she'd built any hopes on a forever sort of relationship with him.

"Shannon, do you want me to get it?" he asked again.

She gave her head a little shake. "No. She's my mother. My problem. But be prepared. You know what she's going to think."

"That we're sleeping together ... oh, no, what's the term you used? *Boinking.*" He practically sneered the word. "She's going to think we're boinking."

"What's with you this morning?" Shannon asked. Enough was enough. "You've been in a mood since we first woke up. Maybe you're regretting last night, but you don't have to worry. I won't be making any demands on you. You set the ground rules and I'm more than happy to live by them. A quick tumble in bed isn't going to change my desire to remain independent."

"Go get the door, Shannon. I'll finish making the coffee and we can talk about my mood and your potential demands after your company leaves."

"Fine." She walked to the door with all the enthusiasm of a woman walking to the guillotine.

Nate was regretting last night. He was probably going to tell her he wanted out of the charade and out of their friendship.

She could get by without ever playing Roxy again, but if Nate left for good... she'd miss him.

Darn.

And if that weren't enough of a problem, her mother was here.

What else could go wrong today?

She opened the door, suddenly very aware of her bare feet.

Why having bare feet should embarrass her, she wasn't sure. Odds were her mother had seen her feet bare thousands of times. But there it was.

Bare feet spoke of comfort... of being relaxed.

Her feet were bare and Nate was in her kitchen making coffee.

No, the day wasn't looking overly bright.

"Good morning, Mom. What's up?"

Brigit pushed her way into the foyer. "Shannon Bonnie O'Malley, that man is here."

"Yes, he is. I think he's in the kitchen finishing making coffee. Would you like a cup?"

"No. It's eight o'clock on a Sunday morning and there's a man in your kitchen making coffee. Do you see what's wrong with this picture?"

"Yes." Shannon nodded, trying to look appropriately serious. "I know what's wrong with this picture, Mom. I'm not in the kitchen drinking that coffee, and you know I function better with a jolt of caffeine coursing through my veins."

"Now, Shannon, I realize you're a grown woman—"

"Do you mom?" Shannon asked softly.

"Do I what?"

"Realize I'm a grown woman?"

"Of course I do. You and your sister are both grown women, and you know the last thing I want to do is interfere in your lives."

"Then why are you here yelling about a man in my kitchen? Why have you spent too many weeks trying to find me a husband? Why—"

Her next *why* would have to wait. There was another knock on the door.

"Did you leave Dad outside?" Shannon asked.

That would be just like her mom. Leaving her father outside left Shannon without an ally. Her mother liked to use every advantage.

"No, I left him at home. He doesn't know that you and Nate are practically living together. It would break the poor man's heart to know that his daughter is shacking up with a man."

"I'm not shacking up. But if it's not Dad, then who…" Shannon left the question trail off as she opened the door and found herself face to face with Nate's mom.

"Mrs. Calder?" she asked weakly.

"Is Nate here?"

"Nate?" Shannon's mom said. "Oh, you mean Bull."

"Bull?" Mrs. Calder echoed, obviously confused.

"Nate's biker name," Shannon's mom supplied.

"That darned motorcycle," Mrs. Calder said as she walked into the house. "I hate it. He's going to get in an accident and kill himself on that thing. Why, he almost did himself in fixing my sink. A man who could injure himself under a sink is a man who shouldn't be tooling around town on a motorcycle. Really, I hate it."

Her mom nodded. "I imagine you do. Look at the slippery slope it dragged Bull down."

Mrs. Calder shot her mom a strange look.

Shannon felt like Alice slipped down the rabbit hole and confronting *Tweedle JuDEE* and *Tweedle Mum.*

Her mom thought Nate was a biker, his mom thought she was a stripper.

If last night's dinner meeting was ill-met, then this morning's gathering was absolutely insane.

"Let me go get Nate," she said weakly.

She needed help here.

Where was he? It didn't take this long to make coffee. He was probably hiding. Well, he could just un-hide because while she might be willing to face her mom on her own, no way was she taking on his as well.

"Why don't you both make yourself at home, while I go find Nate."

"No need," he said as he padded down the hall. He'd obviously helped himself to a quick shower. He was wearing his jeans from the night before, and one of her old t-shirts. What was a big sloppy t-shirt on her, was tight and emphasized every muscle on his chest.

Now that Shannon had firsthand knowledge of that chest, the memory made her blood heat up.

"Mom," he said, "And Mrs. O'Malley. It's a bit early to come calling don't you think?"

"I tried phoning your cellphone," Nate's mom said, "But all I got was your voice mail."

"How did you know where Shannon lives, Mom?" Nate asked.

"I looked it up," she said, then turned to Shannon. "It's easy enough to find online. You should really do something about that."

Shannon reached out and took Nate's hand. Whatever annoyance was between them this morning was forgotten as they joined forces to face their common enemies.

Two enemies at once—before coffee—was too much.

He gave her a reassuring squeeze.

"Shannon," her mother said, "Bull's mother is right. I didn't realize you were that easy to find. Any of your students could call you at home."

"Students?" Mrs. Calder echoed. "Students. That's a good thing to call them, I guess. They all have so much to learn, which is why I want to start—"

Nate interrupted her. "Mom, what did you need me for?"

"Oh, yes. Mick called. He said you were supposed to meet him this morning at seven for some fishing thing?"

"I entirely forgot." He turned to Shannon. "We had a fishing date with a bunch of college buddies."

"They're waiting for you, down on the bay," his mom said.

"Now, about that coffee," her mom said.

"That sounds lovely," Mrs. Calder said. "I'd love a chance to get to know you."

Shannon didn't want her mother and Mrs. Calder sharing confidences over coffee. Yet, they were moving toward the kitchen. She tried to think of something to stop them and cleared her throat, sure that some great idea would come to her before she finished.

"*Ack, ack,*" she coughed, stalling for time.

No great idea appeared.

She tried again. "*Ack, ack.*"

Still nothing.

The women stopped in their tracks.

"Shannon, are you all right?" her mother asked.

"*Ack, ack.* I think something's caught in my throat." She started to hack and sputter, along with the coughing. "*Ack, ack.*"

"Shannon?" her mother said, rushing to her side, Mrs. Calder at her heels. "Honey?"

"Nathan, do something," his mother said.

"*Ack, ack, ack, ack...*" she continued.

Nathan smacked her back.

"*Ack, ack...*"

It was working. Both mother's had forgotten about visiting over coffee. They looked concerned as they watched her choke. "*Ack, ack.*"

"Nate!" his mother cried.

He smacked her back harder.

"*Ack, ack...*"

"Nate, I know you think hitting things is the answer to any problem, but I don't think it's working."

Shannon's throat was feeling quite raw, so she stopped hacking and said, "I think it's better. You saved me, Nate."

"See," he said, shooting his mother a rather superior look, "Smacking things does work."

"Honey, are you sure you're okay?" her mom asked.

"Just let me catch my breath," she said hoarsely.

As Shannon bent over, trying to appear as if she was recuperating from her *choking* spell, she noticed that not only was Nate's tattoo fading, it had a few huge streaks through it.

It obviously was a fake and only a matter of time until her mother spotted it. Spotting details was something her mom was good at.

"Listen, I better get down to the bay before the guys leave me. Thanks for letting me know, Mom," Nate said, herding his mother toward the door.

"About that coffee?" his mom asked.

"I think you two should take a rain check. I need to get going, and Shannon had better go gargle with something."

"What if she starts choking again?" her mom asked.

"Oh, whatever it was, Nate's smacking dislodged it. I'm fine. We'll all just have that coffee another time."

Nate, her hero, was ushering their moms toward the door. "I'll call you this week, Mom."

"Me, too," Shannon assured her mother.

"But—"

"Thanks for stopping," they both said in unison and Nate practically pushed both moms out the door.

Shannon shut it before they could protest.

"Phew," she said.

"Yeah, phew," he echoed.

"So, you better get going if you're going to meet the guys to go fishing."

"Are you sure you don't mind?"

"Mind? Why would I mind? The idea of our being together is that we don't have any real claims on each other. We're together when it's convenient. This is uncomplicated, remember?"

"Yeah, boink-buddies," he said, a hint of that something in his tone that sounded almost like annoyance.

"Yes," she said. "Boink-buddies. Now, get out of here."

"Fine. I'll call you, okay?"

"Sure." She kissed his cheek, a smile on her face.

She kept it plastered there until he left and then allowed it to slip. She had no idea what was wrong with her. This was the perfect relationship.

Uncomplicated.

Dating, but-not-really.

She could have her chick-flicks and a good boinking now and then, too.

Add to that her mom was off her back.

So, why was she feeling so out-of-sorts?

CHAPTER NINE

Shannon took her break outside Monday afternoon, just like every other teacher.

Winters in Erie were long and cold, and spring days were meant to be treasured.

Nate had called after he'd got back from fishing.

Shannon hadn't expected him to, and had felt pleased … too pleased.

Because if she'd felt that happy hearing from him, how would she feel if she hadn't heard?

Miserable.

She was pretty sure that you weren't supposed to feel miserable if you didn't hear from a casual boink-buddy.

After all, the whole point of their dating relationship was that they had the luxury of not calling.

So what was wrong with her?

She didn't have time to figure it out because she had other things to deal with. Patricia was making a beeline toward her, looking determined.

Shannon knew that she was about to be grilled about the scene in the restaurant. She'd known it was coming and had tried to prepare a plan. She'd decided to go on the offensive. Rather than try and explain her outfit she was going on the attack.

The petite brunette with the big curiosity approached the bench, but before she could start her interrogation, Shannon asked, "Patricia, how could you?"

"How could I what?" Patricia looked confused as she sat down next to Shannon.

"How could you not tell me that you and Kyle are dating? I mean, we're friends and friends are supposed to share things like that."

"Well, you were so excited about your date that it just slipped my mind," Patricia said.

It sounded plausible, but Shannon caught the look of guilt that flitted across Patricia's face.

Oh, it was brief, but she saw it.

"Ha! You were hiding the fact you two are dating, even from me."

"Well, let's talk about hiding things," Patricia said. "You made out like you were just excited about a date, when in actuality, you were so happy because you were going out with the man you love."

She paused, as if expecting Shannon to respond, but Shannon couldn't think of a thing to say. She'd expected to be grilled about her outfit, not about being in love.

Because she wasn't in love.

Of course she wasn't.

"You're in love," Patricia repeated as if she could hear Shannon's mental denial. "And you didn't even tell me." She added a huge *humph* to the end of the sentence for punctuation.

"I…" Shannon found it hard to finish the sentence.

The words didn't seem to want to come out, but she forced the issue and hoped Patricia didn't hear the strain in her tone as she finished, "I am not."

Patricia laughed. "Are to."

She shook her head. "You're mistaken. Nate and I are buddies."

Boink-buddies, she thought, but she didn't say that part out loud. There was no reason to give Patricia any more fuel to add to the fire she was building.

"Buddies? I saw how you looked at him. That was more than a *buddy* look."

What happened to her offensive?

Time to get this back on track. "Listen, about you and Kyle—"

"Uh, uh, uh. I'll tell you all about me dating Kyle, but only after you fill me in on what's going on between you and this Nate. And that explanation had better include why you were dressed in those leather pants."

Ah, here was the outfit comment she'd been expecting.

"They weren't leather," Shannon admitted. "*Pleather.* And I highly suggest avoiding the material at all costs, at least when you're going out on a hot date."

Remembering our pleather-experience, she smiled.

"Aha!" Patricia shouted. "There it was. You were thinking of him."

"What?"

"That smile. It says, *ooh-look-at-me-I'm-in-love.*" She leaned closer to Shannon and said, "So, spill it."

And though it was the last thing she'd planned, Shannon did. By the time their break had ended, she'd told Patricia the whole story.

"Wow. That's romantic," Patricia said with a small sigh. "And more than a bit ironic."

"Ironic?" Shannon echoed.

Moronic.

That's how the tale sounded as she told it.

After all, she was an adult. Why on earth would she need to go to such elaborate lengths to foil her mother's plans?

The truth was, she hadn't needed to.

So why had she agreed to this zany plan with Nate?

Because there had been something about him. They'd laughed as they shared their horror stories about their moms. They'd laughed even more as they'd plotted their mutual escapes.

Being with Nate had felt right.

More than right, it had felt—

"You and Nate got together to avoid just this."

"Just what?" Shannon asked, her attention snapping away from her feelings for Nate and back to her friend.

"This. Falling in love." Patricia heaved a mighty sigh and actually put her hand on her chest.

"You've got it all wrong. We didn't want to avoid falling in love, we wanted to avoid our mothers' plans."

"And you fell in love instead," Patricia maintained, punctuating the sentence with another sigh.

"We're not in love."

"Listen, *Roxy*," Patricia said with what sounded suspiciously like a giggle. "You can deny it all you want, but I know love when I see it, and you're in love."

"But—but—" Shannon sputtered.

She didn't love Nate.

After all, they'd only known each other a few weeks.

Of course, she liked spending time with him. From that first meeting she'd felt somehow connected to him.

And maybe she missed him more than a bit when they weren't together. But that didn't mean she was in love.

Did it?

"I'm not looking for that kind of relationship," she said.

"Shannon, love isn't something you can plan on," Patricia continued. "It just is what it is. You love Nate."

"I love Nate?" Shannon whispered weighing the way the words felt as she said them.

They felt almost good.

Right.

She loved Nate?

She loved Nate.

How on earth had she not known that she'd fallen in love with him?

"I love Nate," she stated rather than asked.

"Yes, you do," Patricia said with a grin. "So what are you going to do about it?"

Now, that was a question.

She loved Nate, a man looking for an uncomplicated relationship.

And suddenly what they had together was looking more than just a bit complicated.

What was she going to do?

Nate looked frazzled.

More than that, he looked ready to pull his hair out as he listened to something someone was saying on the phone. Shannon stood at the counter, waiting for him to notice her. When he did, he smiled and held up a finger for her to wait.

"...No, ma'am. It's not meant to be taken orally. It's a suppository. It goes..."

He finished his explanation and Shannon felt a stab of pity for him. After all, it had to be an uncomfortable thing to explain.

He hung up and gave Shannon a weak smile. "Hey."

"Bad day?" she asked.

"You don't know the half of it. I'm used to odd questions and can handle most without blinking an eye, but today it's been one odd thing after another. I had to explain that birth control pills have to be taken *every* day, not just on days you have sex. And then there was the couple who—" He stopped. "No sense in depressing us both. So, what brings you in today?"

"Maybe I have a prescription?" she asked, teasing in her voice, hoping to make him smile, she added, "Or maybe I just wanted to see you."

That was the truth.

Since the moment the light bulb had gone off this afternoon, she'd been anxious to see him and decide if she was right, if she really loved this man.

She stared at him and tried to measure what she felt... and she couldn't. It was so big and all encompassing, that it couldn't be quantified.

It was limitless.

Only one emotion could be that big.

Love.

Yes, she loved Nathan Calder.

So now what?

Did she blurt out *I love you*, or did she wait and try to simply work it into a conversation?

Hey, Nate, you never stall your motorcycle any more... and by the way, I think I love you.

She groaned.

No, she was simply going to have to wait to tell him until she could think of a better approach.

"Is something wrong?" he asked. "Did my mom come back?"

"No, nothing's wrong, exactly. I thought maybe you'd like dinner?"

Dinner.

She could tell him at dinner. After all, it was better to just say the words and get it over with.

She wasn't going to worry about form or style. She wouldn't even worry about changing the rules. She would just say those three words, *I love you* and trust that it would all work out.

Yes, she'd tell him tonight at dinner.

"Dinner sounds good. I need a quiet night more than you know. The idea of a quiet, uncomplicated evening is ever so appealing."

Shannon almost flinched at the word *uncomplicated*.

She was pretty sure saying she loved him wouldn't constitute an uncomplicated night. After all, loving him changed everything. And everyone knew that change was always complicated.

She wasn't going to tell him.

Maybe he'd simply sense it. After all, how could he miss it? She felt as if she had a sign flashing over her head... *I love Nate... I love Nate...*

How could he miss something like that?

She'd make long, slow love to him and he'd know. Ah, now that was a plan. Even if he didn't sense it, she'd still get to make love to him. Not boinking.

She smiled at the thought and said, "Well, we'll have to see if we can find something to do that will relieve your stress."

"Oh, that sounds like a plan," he said, and murmured a few specifics in her ear.

"Nate," she whispered back, feeling breathless and tingly all over.

If she let him do what he was planning to do, she could whisper the *words I love you* in his ear.

Maybe he'd even whisper them right back.

She could only imagine how much more breathless and tingly she'd be over that.

That's it, she was going to tell him.

"I'm so glad you stopped by," he continued. "I mean, everyone wants something from me, all day long. It's Nate-this, and Nate-that. Give me something as undemanding as what we have and life is good."

Undemanding.

That was as horrible a word as *uncomplicated.*

If she said *I love you* maybe he'd feel obligated to say the words back.

That would definitely be demanding.

Darn. She wasn't going to tell him.

At least not tonight.

She wanted the perfect moment to say the words. The perfect night.

Tonight didn't sound like the time.

No, she wasn't going to tell him.

Before she could answer, someone called, "Nate."

"'Scuse me," he said, hurrying toward the back of the pharmacy.

She watched him go, the feeling in her chest growing, beating to get out and she wondered how she could go through an entire night looking at him, listening to him, laughing with him and not tell him how she felt. The feeling was that big.

Even if she didn't plan on telling him, it might slip out.

Then things would get complicated and he'd feel as if she was demanding and then he'd never say the words back.

It was an excuse and she knew it, but even if she'd figured out she was in love with Nate, she wasn't quite sure what to do with those feelings.

She had to sort things out.

Feeling decidedly like a coward, she looked at the clerk and said, "Just tell Nathan that I…"

She hesitated, trying to think of a plausible lie, and settled for a half-truth.

"Tell him that I can see he's busy. Tell him to forget about dinner and go relax. I'll talk to him…soon. Tomorrow."

She hurried out before he could come back and find her and ask questions. Because she didn't feel that she had any answers at all.

Nate had been disappointed Monday when he came out of the backroom and found that Shannon had gone. Seeing her had made his day-from-hell brighten considerably.

But she'd run out and canceled dinner.

Why?

Maybe his bad mood had scared her off. After all, they had an informal relationship, one based on fun. His mood wasn't fun. But it had been such a stressful day, and talking with her had made him feel better.

Just seeing her walk in the store and smile had been enough to make him feel better.

Then she left.

It wasn't just that it was one of those days when things went wrong, it was one of those days where nothing went right.

When Shannon left things went from bad to worse. He needed her. It was a feeling that was growing by leaps and bounds.

He was addicted to her, he decided.

And it wasn't an addiction he was looking to break.

Her boink-buddy comment had annoyed him because it wasn't accurate. They were more than that, even if she didn't want to admit it.

At least, she was more than that to him. He hoped he was more than that to her.

How much more?

That was the question that had been plaguing him.

How much more was she to him? How much more did he want to be to her?

He'd called her that night hoping he could convince her he was in a better mood. He was eager to see her, to explore just what they had become. But Shannon said she had to go to her mom's.

He asked if she wanted him to come as well, but she'd said no. She had it under control.

Tuesday he had hockey practice, so he suggested they get together Wednesday night.

Thursday they'd talked a few minutes, but couldn't get together because she'd promised to go out with her friend Patricia.

But to be honest, that wasn't the question that was nagging him. No, he was worried about why she avoiding him, because he was pretty sure she was.

He wasn't taking any chances on Friday.

He hadn't seen her since Monday, and on Monday it had been a brief glimpse at best. Not nearly enough.

He missed her.

Which is why he parked his Harley in front of her house and hurried to the door.

He hadn't called first. Mainly because he was just hearing her voice, or simply grabbing a few seconds with her.

Oh, he knew they'd set the ground rules. This was supposed to be an easygoing sort of relationship. One where they saw each other when they had the time and the inclination. There were no strings.

But he'd had the inclination all week, and would have made the time, but Shannon had been busy.

Too busy for him. Not needing to see him as much as he needed to see her.

To hear her.

To touch her.

He was thinking about touching her as he rapped on the door.

She opened it, wearing as anti-Roxy an outfit as she possibly could. Well-worn grey sweats, a battered t-shirt, short spiky hair wild ... and he'd never seen a woman look more lovely. More tantalizing.

More ...

He'd planned at least saying, *Hi, Shannon,* and playing it casual, following the absurd rules they'd set down, but when as he drank in the sight of her, the only thing he wanted to do was ...

He pulled her into his arms and kissed her.

Not just some little peck-on-the-cheek-sort-of-greeting.

No.

It was long and hot with desire.

He kicked the door shut with his foot, and pulled his jacket off, without breaking the contact.

He eased her around the corner and into living room.

He turned and let himself fall onto the couch, pulling her along with him.

She landed on his chest.

"Nate, is this going to be big enough?"

Even though his brain was muddled with the feel of Shannon, he knew she was asking if the couch was big enough to hold them both, but he deliberately misconstrued the question. "It was big enough last time."

"But we didn't do it here..." she said, then let the sentence fade off as she caught his entendre and started to laugh as she said, "It was more than big enough. It was huge. It was massive. Oh, I shouldn't go on like this, or I'll give you a swollen head."

"Too late," he said, as he burst out laughing. They both laughed until they were breathless with it.

Their quips were funny, but not quite that funny. For Nate, the laughter was just a giddy sort of release. He was here, with Shannon, where he belonged.

This.

Just that one word summed up why he'd spent the week missing Shannon.

This.

He felt complete, holding her, laughing with her.

And as he showed her that a couch could indeed be *big enough*, he knew *this* was much more than boinking.

This wasn't uncomplicated, as they'd planned.

As a matter of fact, he suspected *this* could be quite complicated. He didn't mind the complication at all, and hoped he could convince Shannon not to mind as well.

They twisted and somehow managed to snuggle on the couch afterward.

"Nate, I—" Shannon started, then stopped herself short.

He waited for her to finish the sentence. She finally said, "I just wanted to say, you were right, it was plenty big enough."

She laughed then, and gently ran a finger along his jawline.

It was just the smallest of caresses, but it was enough to stir Nate's desire.

"Maybe we should go get a shower and then finish discussing how big is big enough," he said with a chuckle.

"Now, that's an offer a girl can't refuse."

They raced to the shower, laughing like a couple of kids.

Nate knew he'd have to tell her that things had changed for him, that he didn't want to be boink-buddies, he wanted more.

He wanted it all.

Tomorrow morning he'd tell her everything.

CHAPTER TEN

"Good morning," Nate murmured in her ear.

Shannon snuggled closer to him, not saying anything, mainly because her first impulse was to blurt out those words she'd decided not to blurt—at least not until she could figure out just how to say them right.

If she said them wrong he might leave. After all, love isn't what he signed on for ... *uncomplicated* was.

Nate was toying with her hair as he held her tight.

She liked the way it felt.

Wrapped in Nate.

Waking up on a Saturday morning with him in her bed.

She'd missed him so much this week, but had stayed away because she was afraid ... afraid she'd blurt out the words and ruin everything.

The words were right there on the end of her tongue, but she valiantly held them in, not wanting to scare him off.

"Are you just going to lie there all morning?" he asked with a chuckle.

Pushing the words to the back of her mouth, she managed to squeeze, "Maybe," out past them.

She congratulated herself for not saying them.

Maybe she could be with him and not say them, at least not until there was a chance he'd say them back.

If she could just give him more time maybe he'd love her, too. The thought made her feel annoyed with herself.

But it was true. She did want his love. She didn't think she was cut out for unrequited love.

"Are you hungry?" he asked.

"Yes."

Aha, she'd managed another word and hadn't let those three little ones slip.

She was getting good at this.

"Do you feel like taking a chance on my making pancakes?"

"I love—" She bit the words back and filled in, "—pancakes. I'm more than willing to take a chance on your cooking."

Sneaky, sneaky little words.

Almost as sneaky as the feeling that had stole into her heart and wouldn't let her shake it.

Nate looked almost disappointed for a split second. Maybe he'd hoped she'd offer to cook them?

The look passed quickly, and in its place, he smiled. "Maybe after we fortify our strength with breakfast we could come back in here and ..."

He whispered his plans in her ear. Soft and low, his voice tickled her ear.

She hoped he could make his pancakes fast because his offer sounded very, very tempting.

She nodded, saying, "I love—"

Darn. There they were again. "—I'd love to."

How on earth was she going to have breakfast and then make love to Nate again and not say them?

"Coffee first?"

"That sounds wonderful." A complete sentence with no slips.

Maybe she could handle not telling him how much she loved him, telling him how cute he was on the back of his

Harley, how much she liked hearing about his day, how much she loved spending an evening arguing about what constituted a chick-flick, and how much she loved the sight of him dressed as a Harley rider or as a pharmacist.

She couldn't tell him how much she liked watching him with his parents, how much she loved waking up next to him, how much she loved...just how much she loved him.

She pushed back the words and the thoughts, and pulled back the blanket. She gave a small yip. "It's cold in here."

Nate didn't yip as he crawled out of bed, but she could see goose bumps covering the skin she'd grown to know so well.

Shannon reached in her closet, pulled out her favorite Winnie the Pooh robe and wrapped it around herself. It might be a bit ratty, but it was still warm.

"Here," she said, handing him a second robe, the one her mom had bought her for Christmas and she'd never worn. Her taste didn't match her mothers in robes or much else, for that matter.

She could have offered him something else, but one of the other things she happened to love was teasing Nate.

"It's pink," he grumbled, almost on cue, holding with two fingers as if the color was somehow contagious.

"So?" she countered.

"Real men don't wear pink."

"Would you rather wear Pooh?" she asked.

"I think real men are even less likely to wear Pooh."

"I mean if you're really that insecure about your masculinity, I'll find you something else."

"I'm not insecure." He slipped it on. "But I mean, if I were really Bull, I'd deal with the chill without resorting to this," he muttered as he knotted the belt.

What was a huge robe on her stretched to its limits across Nate's much broader shoulder.

Looking at him, his hair sleep-mussed, wearing her pink robe, Shannon was awash with the need to say the words.

To just let them out.

Forget planning.

Forget perfect.

She was going to be brave and simply say them. She loved so many things about Nate, that she simply couldn't contain it another minute.

Tell him.

That's all she could do. That and pray he wouldn't walk right out the door, but would stick around long enough to learn to love her, too.

Ah, but he was wearing a pink bathrobe. He'd never walk out the door in that.

He was trapped.

This was the perfect time.

"Nate, there's something I have to tell you. I've spent the week trying to decide how, and finally have come to the conclusion that there's no right way. It's something important…" The words that had been aching to come out, hung back.

"Yes?" he said, when the silence hung in the room a few seconds too long for comfort.

Shannon garnered her strength, and said, "I love—"

The doorbell rang.

Who on earth would be ringing her doorbell at eight o'clock on a Saturday morning, interrupting her perfect moment?

"Mom," she muttered. Who else could it be? "I'll get rid of her."

Shannon Bonnie O'Malley, aka Roxy, had had enough. She wasn't going to play dodge-the-wedding-bullet with her mom any more.

She wasn't going to try and find a perfect way to tell the man she loved that she loved him.

She was going to be bold and take charge. She was kicking her mom out and then she was going to talk to Nate. She was going to tell him she loved him and he was just going to have to deal with the complication.

"You want help?" he asked.

"No. You go start the coffee, I'll get rid of her."

He kissed her cheek. "Good luck."

He went to the kitchen and Shannon marched to the front door.

Enough was enough.

She pulled the door open and just stared.

"Good morning, Shannon, dear," Mrs. Calder said.

Her mother leaned over and kissed her cheek. "Good morning, sweetheart. Judy and I met in the driveway. You know what they say, great minds think alike. I brought donuts."

"And I baked some homemade muffins this morning," Mrs. Calder said.

Shannon decided both moms visiting again was scarier than the thought of Mrs. Calder's homemade muffins.

She tried to think of something to say, "I ... uh ..."

Her resolve might have been enough to let her deal with her mother, but no amount of resolve could deal with both mothers.

She needed reinforcements.

She needed Nate.

"Come on in, Judy," her mom said as she and Mrs. Calder walked past Shannon and into the house.

"Is Nate still in bed?" her mom asked, without waiting for an answer.

Shannon heard Nate say, "Mom," as the two women walked into the kitchen.

Knowing there was nothing to do but follow, Shannon did just that. She realized that her feet were bare, but she couldn't even work up any embarrassment about it.

She simply had too much on her mind and three little words just dying to be said, but there was no way to say them with both their mothers here.

"Shannon, your mom brought donuts and mine made us muffins," Nate said, a grim mock-smile pasted on his lips.

"Yes, they told me."

"So, what brings you both out this early on a Saturday morning?" he asked both mothers as he poured coffee into four mugs.

"I came to tell Shannon she had to quit her job," his mom said. "I worry all the time. This can't go on, and I'm sure her mother agrees with me."

"Quit her job? Of course I don't agree with you. At least Shannon has steady work and a steady paycheck. While all your son does is ride around on a motorcycle all day."

"I hate that motorcycle," his mom confessed.

The phone rang and Shannon automatically picked it up. "Hello?"

"Shannon," Kate said. "I'm thinking I should come home. Mom says that this Bull guy is trouble and..."

The argument about motorcycles and quitting jobs continued.

Kate poured out her worries across the phone line.

Nate stood there looking as lost as Shannon felt.

Shannon realized that telling Nate she loved him couldn't possibly get any more complicated than this.

The teacher in her came to life. Shannon put her fingers to her lips and let out a shrill whistle ... *Zwwwwwippppp.*

Three sets of eyes were immediately focused on her.

She'd known they would be. She'd used the whistle for years to get unruly students' attention.

"Enough!" she said.

She put the phone to her ear and said, "Kate, I'll call you back later. Don't come home. Everything's under control."

"Mom and Mrs. Calder, I'm done playing games. Things aren't the way they seem. This is…"

She looked to Nate and saw he gave a small nod of agreement. "It all started at Mick's bar, just like we said. It was after one of the horrendous dates you fixed me up on, Mom. I'd had enough."

"Me, too, Mom," Nate said. "All that, *And I almost died giving birth to you, and all I want is a grandbaby…* stuff. And fixing me up with some initial girl."

"Kay," his mother supplied.

"Yeah, fixing up," Shannon echoed. "Remember Shelby, Mom? Shelby and Shannon. At least if someone said Nate and Kay it wouldn't sound like you were being shushed in a library."

Nate laughed. "I hadn't thought of that, but you're right. You aren't destined for a Shelby."

"Shannon has definite ideas about what names go together," her mother said. "Nate and Shannon. Those go well, don't you think dear?"

Shannon couldn't begin to tell her mother just how much she agreed… at least not until she told Nate how much they went together.

"That's our point, Shannon and Nate don't really go together, at least not the way you two think."

"Or Roxy and Bull," Mrs. Calder said. "Those two names go well together, too, don't you think, Brigit?"

"I certainly do, Judy."

They knew.

Their mother's knew the truth.

Shannon saw it in their eyes.

"But as much as my daughter focuses on names," her mom continued, "I have to say, I prefer focusing on careers, on personal traits. And I'd say a pharmacist and a teacher go together about as well as—"

"A biker and a stripper—"

"Exotic dancer." Nate corrected his mom before Shannon could.

Shannon reached out, took his hand and gave it a squeeze. "So you both know this is just an act."

"Of course we knew. We're bright, capable women who saw through your little charade," his mom said.

Shannon's mom gave her a funny look. "But it's not all an act."

"What do you mean?" she asked.

"Why look at the two of you, united against us. Holding hands, sleeping over. You two are in love," her mom said, her voice practically cooing. She sounded just the way Patricia had.

"I can't speak for Nate, but how I feel for him isn't something I'm going to discuss with the two of you. As a matter of fact, it's time you both left. You've meddled enough. Nate and I will work things out on our own."

"But, honey, there are just some things that a girl needs her mother for."

"You're right, Mom, but this isn't one of them." She steered both protesting mothers to the door. "Thank you for stopping by."

"But—" her mother and Mrs. Calder said in unison.

"But nothing. Nate and I are adults. Whatever is going to happen next in our relationship is up to us."

"This isn't about the bet, you know, honey," her mom said softly. "I want you to be happy. I think Nate's the man for you."

"I know that, Mom." She kissed her mother's cheek.

Shannon shut the door on both of the moms, then headed back to the kitchen.

She hoped that when she said the words Nate would admit he loved her as well, or that he was willing to give them a chance.

"They're gone?" he asked.

"Yes."

"Phew," he wiped his brow. "We may be able to handle keeping things uncomplicated, but our moms certainly try to make things interesting. Do you think they'll stay off our backs now that they know the truth."

"No," she said with a small smile. "They'll probably both start in again tomorrow."

"So…" he paused, obviously looking for something to say, "Do you still want those pancakes?" he asked.

"No, I don't think so."

"You said you wanted to talk about something?"

"I…" She was chickening out. There he was, standing in the middle of her kitchen, and all she wanted to do was run over to him and shout the words, *I love you.*

She gathered her courage.

Before she could get the words out he said, "Just because they know doesn't mean our…" he hesitated, obviously looking a description of their relationship.

"Our dating-but-not-really relationship?" she asked. "Our boink-buddy-ness? Our *uncomplicated* thing?"

"Yes. There's no reason we can't keep seeing each other. I enjoy being with you. What we have is good."

Talk about being damned by faint praise.

Here she was ready to spill her heart to him, to tell him she was finding it hard to breathe when he wasn't around and he says that he enjoys being with her?

Of course he thought what they had was good. It was uncomplicated.

Shannon hated that word at this point.

She hated this stupid charade.

She'd just say the words, and when he dumped her she'd pick herself up and move on.

Maybe she'd agree to go out with Shelby. After all, he might not be complicated-phobic.

"I don't think things can continue the way they've been going," she started. "After all, part of our reason for being together is gone. Our moms know."

"Still, what we have works, Shannon-me-love..."

"Don't you Shannon-me-love me," she said. "Here I am, ready to spill my heart to you and tell you I love you and your still harping on our stupid deal, our *uncomplicated* plans."

This time she was the one shaking a finger, she shook it right in his face as she continued, "Well, I want complicated. I want it all. I want someone who calls me every day, not just when he feels like. No, I take that back, I want a man who feels like calling me every day. But you don't want that. That would be messy. Well, that's fine. Just fine. I'll go find a man who doesn't mind a bit of complication."

"You think you can replace me that easily?" he asked, softly, moving closer.

"Sure." Which was a big lie. She doubted she'd ever replace Nathan.

"You think you'll find another guy who doesn't mind wearing a pink bathrobe and watching chick-flicks, who knows how to pry you out of pleather...who loves you like I do?"

"I'm sure there are men out there who are secure enough in their masculinity to wear pink and watch chick-flicks. As for pleather—" she stopped, unsure she'd heard what she thought she heard.

"Say that again."

"I know how to pry you out of pleather," he said, a big grin on his face.

"Not that part." She grabbed the fluffy pink material and pulled him close.

"I don't mind watching chick-flicks if they have at least a bit of blood-and-guts. I may wear pink, but I like blood-and-guts."

"Nope. Not that part either." She felt as if she was going to explode with joy.

"Oh. I love you?" he asked with a smile.

"Yep, that's the part."

"I do." He kissed her then and she could feel it.

He did—he loved her.

She broke the kiss and said, "But you were just going on about how you wanted uncomplicated…"

"You didn't want love, you wanted to be boink-buddies."

"No, I didn't. I thought that's what you wanted. I realized the other day that what I feel for you went further than I ever expected it to. I came to the pharmacy to tell you."

"But you ran out on me," he said with a frown.

"You were tired and rattling on about needing things uncomplicated, and I knew saying those words would complicate everything, so I didn't."

"Shannon, nothing in my life has been uncomplicated since I met you. As a matter of fact, this is the most complicated, convoluted relationship I've ever been in … and I couldn't be happier. Or rather, I could be if you did one little thing."

"What's that?" she asked. She'd do anything for him—for the man she loved.

"Say the words. You still haven't said them, you know."

"Really? How negligent of me. Nathan *Bull* Calder, I love you. I think I loved you from that first time we talked at Mick's."

Suddenly she was wrapped in Nate, her face pressed to a fuzzy pink bathrobe. She felt as if she could burst, she was so happy.

"So, you know what this means?" he asked.

"What?"

"Your mom's won her bet."

"No, no she hasn't. The bet was that I'd get married…" She looked up and saw his intent in his eyes. "Oh."

"One more word, that's all I need from you."

"Yes."

"Should we go call our moms? They're probably still in the driveway trying to decide what to do next."

"Later," Shannon said. Her mom would be absolutely beside herself with excitement—and totally unbearable to live with as she tried to plan the wedding.

Shannon remembered how bad it had been when her mom tried to plan Kate's.

"My mom will just have to wait a while longer. There's something we have to do first."

"What would that be?" He ran a finger along her cheek.

It was the slightest touch, but left Shannon decidedly weak in the knees and more than a bit breathless.

"Have I ever mentioned I find men who wear pink very sexy?" she asked, her voice a soft whisper.

"Is that so?"

"Almost as sexy as bikers named Bull."

Laughing, they forgot their moms.

They forgot all about complications.

All they remembered was love.

After all, that was all that really mattered.

Epilogue

"May I present, the brides and grooms," Father Murphy boomed as two couples walked into Sabella's for the reception.

"Kiss. Kiss. Kiss. Kiss," the crowd chanted.

Brigit O'Malley watched as her daughter—her beautiful, talented daughter—kissed her brand new husband.

She sniffed. It was a dainty sniff... quiet and refined.

Not at all like the big honking sniffs Cecilia was making as Cara and her Texan kissed as well.

Cecilia had called weeks ago and told her Cara was getting married. She'd rattled on and on about her wedding plans... plans that never came to fruition.

A part of Brigit had felt bad when Cara and her Texan eloped. She'd almost resigned herself to paying for *that woman's* trip to the Catskills. After all, even without a big wedding, Cecilia won.

And when a daughter ruined all her mother's wedding dreams, a trip was the least of what a mother deserved.

Brigit remembered how she felt when Mary Kathryn had eloped, but when Cecilia starting lording it over Brigit's head, her sympathy ran short.

But Nathan was brilliant. Truly a genius. He pointed out that Cecilia hadn't truly won because a Catholic wasn't truly married without a priest.

No. A civil service didn't count.

She was so lucky he was now her son-in-law.

Of course, she hadn't counted on her traitor daughter.

For some reason, Shannon felt a bond to Cara, although to the best of her knowledge the two had never met. Kate and Cara had become friends, and through her, Shannon and Cara formed a bond. They ended up talking and coming up with this diabolical plan.

Cara and her Rex had shared today's ceremony, having their civil marriage blessed at the same time she and Nate married.

The girls suggested they felt drawn to each other because both their mothers were meddlers.

A meddler?

No way.

Brigit knew she was just a loving, concerned mother.

As was her good friend, Cecilia.

Brigit sighed as the couples moved onto the dance floor. She spotted Kate and Tony. And there was that delightful wedding planner, Desi and Seth. Everyone was here.

She sighed again.

"We did good, didn't we?" Cecilia asked.

Brigit loped her arm around the shorter woman's shoulders. "Yes, we did. They all look so happy."

"Speaking of happy, about the bet…"

Brigit nodded. "Yes, I know it's a draw. The girls planned it that way. Our children are trickier than I ever gave them credit for."

"They take after their mamas."

Brigit smiled. "Yes, I guess they do."

"But I was thinking, maybe we should go."

"Go?"

"To the Catskills together. I talked to Rachel and Jessica-Marie. Rachel's going to be away on business, but

134

Jessica-Marie would love to come. And I thought maybe we'd ask your son-in-law's mama, that Judy Calder, to fill in for our fourth."

"Fourth?"

"Well, we need someone for Pinochle. A long weekend. Think of the games we could have."

"The four of us in the Catskills?" Brigit hugged her friend.

Her best friend.

The kind of friend that only came along once in a lifetime. "Oh, Cecilia, that would be lovely. We'll have so much fun. And we deserve a vacation, after all the work the girls put us through."

"And do we get any thanks?" Cecilia asked.

"No. Why all I asked for was a dignified service and just look at these cakes. They're not what I would have chosen."

Brigit personally thought that despite the fact they were not quite dignified, Shannon's was ever so much nicer than Cara's.

Why Cara had a bull on hers.

Brigit wasn't sure she'd want a bull on top of a cake, but Cara said that it was a bull that brought her and Rex together and then laughed. Brigit didn't get the joke.

But she did get Shannon's cake toppers. A Harley Davidson with two Barbies that Desi and Seth had loaned them. The Ken doll was dressed in black and had a small tattoo on his forearm, and Barbie, she had on tight red leather pants.

Every time she looked at those pants, Shannon laughed, though she wouldn't share the joke with her mother. But Brigit did understand the rest of it.

Instead of saying Shannon and Nate it said, Roxy and Bull.

The stripper and the biker.

Brigit hugged Cecilia. "Yes, after all the work we've gone to, making sure the kids were happily married, I think we need a break. The Catskills it is."

"Great, because soon I won't be able to get away."

"Why?" Brigit asked.

"Because I'm sure my Cara and her Rex will be giving me a grandbaby soon."

"Nate's mother was just telling me that she plans to be a grandmother early next year, something about Nate owing her a baby since he almost killed her. She seemed positive, so I'm sure I'll be a grandmother before you."

"You want to bet?" Cecilia asked.

Brigit looked at the reception room full of people she loved. Now that both her girls were happily married, it was time to add to the family again.

She smiled. "You're on ..."

Dear Reader,

I hope you enjoyed this sequel to *How to Catch a Groom*. *How to Hunt a Husband's* Shannon and Nate had a unique way of coping with meddling mothers. It was so much fun. I'll confess, I love going to work every day because I get to spend my work-hours with characters like *Roxy* and *Bull*.

If you enjoyed the story, would you please go leave a review at your favorite online site? Those reviews help others find the book!

As always, thank you for all your support!

Holly

Award-winning author Holly Jacobs has over three million books in print worldwide. The first novel in her Everything But... series, *Everything But a Groom*, was named one of 2008's Best Romances by Booklist, and her books have been honored with many other accolades. She lives in Erie, Pennsylvania, with her husband and four children. You can visit her at *www.HollyJacobs.com*.

Other Holly Jacobs Books for Your Kindle

Romance and Romantic Comedy Single Titles
Briar Hill Road
The Moments (a short story sequel to Briar Hill Road
Just One Thing
Same Time Next Summer
Not Precisely Pregnant
Can't Find NoBODY
Hung Up On You
I Waxed My Legs for This?
Her Second-Chance Family

Words of the Heart series
Book 1 Carry Her Heart
Book 2 These Three Words
Book 3 Hold Her Heart
Book4 Between the Words

PTA Moms Trilogy
Book 1 Once Upon a Thanksgiving
Books 2 Once Upon a Christmas
Book 3 Once Upon a Valentine's

Cupid Falls series
Book 1 Christmas in Cupid Falls
Book 2 A Simple Heart: A Cupid Falls Novella

Dear Fairy Godmother ... series
Book 1 Mad About Max
Book 2 Magic for Joy
Book 3 Miracles for Nick
Book 4 Fairly Human

Everything But ... series
Book 1 Everything But a Groom
Book 2 Everything But a Bride
Book 3 Everything But a Wedding
Book 4 Everything But a Christmas Eve
Book 5 Everything But a Mother
Book 6 Everything But a Dog

Maid in L.A. Mystery series
Book 1 Steamed
Book 2 Dusted
Book 3 Spruced Up
Book 4 Swept Up

Perry Square series (A Holly Jacobs Classic)
Book 1 Do You Hear What I Hear?
Book 2 A Day Late and a Bride Short
Book 3 Dad Today, Groom Tomorrow
Book 4 Be My Baby
Book 5 Once Upon a Princess

Book 6 Once Upon a Prince
Book 7 Once Upon a King
Book 8 Here With Me

WLVH Series:
Book 1 Pickup Lines
Book 2 Lovehandles
Book 3 Night Calls
Book 4 Laugh Lines

Whedon Series
Book 1 Unexpected Gifts
Book 2 A One-of-a-Kind Family
Book 3 Homecoming Day
Book 4 A Father's Name

Valley Ridge Series
Book 1 You Are Invited ...
Book 2 April Showers
Book 3 A Walk Down the Aisle
Book 4 A Valley Ridge Christmas

Short Stories and Novellas
The Book
Labor Day
There He Was
13 Weeks
Bosom Buddies
Cinderella Wore Tennis Shoes
Able to Love Again

Nothing But Series
Book 1 Nothing But Love
Book 2 Nothing But Heart
Book 3 Nothing But Luck

Love all the books? Try a bundle or boxset!
Short Stories for the Overworked and Under-Read Anthology
Maid in L.A. Mysteries Bundle
PTA Mom Collection

Made in United States
North Haven, CT
18 June 2025

69936624R00085